T0148327

Phantom of the Frog Hop

A Novelette

BIG BAND YEARS,
A DRAMA OF ENDEARMENT

LEE EMERSON GINGERY

iUniverse, Inc.
New York   Bloomington

Phantom of the Frog Hop
A Novelette. BIG BAND YEARS, A DRAMA OF ENDEARMENT

iUniverse books may be ordered through booksellers or by contacting:

iUniverse
1663 Liberty Drive
Bloomington, IN 47403
www.iuniverse.com
1-800-Authors (1-800-288-4677)

ISBN: 978-1-4502-4060-4 (pbk)
ISBN: 978-1-4502-4061-1 (ebk)

Printed in the United States of America

iUniverse rev. date: 10/1/2010

Introduction

Between the covers of this book are a novelette, three *short,* Short Stories plus nine shorter anecdotal narratives of modest size. A few of these shorter pieces describe interesting people and events we deem worthy of sharing. Most document some experiences or observations that chronicle glimpses of our life and times in 20th Century America. Having been sheltered the first two decades of my life in tiny Rushville, Missouri… (though since 1960 my wife and I have lived in Shenandoah, Iowa.) I was, in a sense, tempered, perhaps touched, by serving in combat in World War II. Therefore some of these shorter subjects are personal travel sojourns, or in a broader context, perhaps, life adventures that my family and I have lived and often cherished. So I am driven to share these times, illustrating my interpretation, of these personalities or moments. All four of the longer expositions in the beginning of this book are, largely, products of my imagination.

Thank You,
Lee Emerson Gingery

Contents

PHANTOM OF THE FROG HOP
Prologue

Who would have dreamed that the finest ballroom in the American Midwest would be built in Saint Joseph, Missouri in the nineteen twenties? At the time, Saint Joseph was the third largest city in the state of Missouri after Saint Louis and Kansas City. Population was about 80,000, with its growth and progress evident, but not remarkable, dating back to the latter part of the nineteenth century.

Earlier in 1859 a rail line, largely financed by the state of Missouri, was completed across northern Missouri terminating at the settlement first called Blacksnake Hills but soon wisely renamed Saint Joseph. At that time the population was estimated at about 9,000 homesteaders. It soon was assumed that influential government officials, and certain political leaders agreed that the rail line should follow the river south to Kansas City instead of crossing the Missouri River at Saint Joseph. The young community lacked the requisite politically powerful personages to mandate that the railroad push west across the river at that location. Despite this, the city became the premier municipality in northern Missouri. Its trade territory soon extended well beyond Buchanan County where it quickly became the county seat. The city's businesses and industries found regular patrons as far north as the Iowa line a hundred miles away and more than twice that distance east, and also west across the river (via primitive ferries) into Kansas. Saint Joseph shared the trade territory to the south with Kansas City which was figured to be a little more than fifty miles away. The people living in and around the city of Saint Joseph were industrious and resourceful. Most reflected the genteel, friendly good manners of their forebears who had migrated to northwest Missouri from the mid south states of Kentucky and Tennessee.

Also, not a few foreign immigrants found St. Joseph a fertile place to put down roots. Many hailed from the British Iles, Germany and northern Europe. For instance, two of this author's ancestors emigrated from Scotland and settled in the environs of Saint Joseph in the year 1869.

So how did that city acquire a ball room? The miracle happened because in the mid nineteen twenties there lived a man named Frank A. Frogge residing beyond the east city limits of Saint Joseph who was possessed of such a dream. Actually it was his enthusiasm, resources and drive that made the project become a *fait accompli*. Solely with the force of his often eccentric, rough and tumble, "don't take no for an answer" personae, Frogge designed and built the huge ballroom. He had the concept but he also did a little research. Along with two close confidantes, Frogge chose to visit important ballrooms in Kansas City, Chicago and Des Moines, Iowa. He had also heard of a Democratic Party convention that took place in Houston, Texas in an enormous hall. He traveled to Houston in 1928 and learned that the structure there boasted what was called a Lamella roof which could shelter an area of 160 by 200 square feet of space. Most importantly, by using the Lamella roof design, his proposed ballroom would not require any pillars or columns for support, allowing most of that space for the dance floor.

Frogge, (pronounced using the long "o") who actually liked to be called "Frog," was a truck gardener, hauler, owner of a construction company and, most importantly, a vision-ary /entrepreneur. By the mid- twenties he had sired eleven children and apparently provided a good living for the large family all of whom supported him in this new endeavor. With the advent of the early swing music era, Frank knew Saint Joseph needed a nice ballroom that would attract the bands and dancers, as he loved the new swing music. Thus he set about to build his dream.

Locating the site involved give and take with family and close friends. But Frogge owned some land where Pickett Road joins what became the Belt Highway, outside the city limits of Saint Joseph. That plot of land would be commodious enough for the ballroom, an attached restaurant and vehicle parking. However there would be no available water, and electricity was not totally reliable. But the nearby flowing spring could be enlarged to supply ample water and a generator would be built to provide sufficient electrical power. Ambience was also enhanced by the existence of a nearby orchard. With these de-cisions finalized, that very site was chosen and the first stakes were soon driven prior to preparing the foundation.

Summoning the local expert craftsmen required to lay the widely praised floor, was one of his first fortuitous moves. Decorating the interior was an amalgam of brain storming ideas. The colors chosen were appropriately muted neutral shades. Years later the decorating included the "trademark" silver leaves, a clever idea unequaled anywhere else at that time. The visual impact was striking as the decorative leaves seemed to be shimmering in a breeze above the heads of the dancers. From the beginning, name bands who were booked to play for the crowds unanimously declared that the acoustics from the bandstand were absolutely perfect.

Nearing the final stages of construction Frank had not yet chosen an appropriate name for his brain child. After various suggestions were advanced, he settled on using his "nickname" of Frog which would be combined with that local ubiquitous hopping amphibian. Thus the new venture would be called *The Frog Hop Ballroom…*

Frogge and a close friend whom he had named on-site manager of the ballroom set their sights aiming for a grand opening on the night of December 31st,1928…New Year's Eve. The opening night band had been signed: Claude Bruce's Troubadours. For several weeks in advance, advertising appeared in the Saint Joseph News Press announcing the New Year's Eve dance at the new "$50,000 Frog Hop Ballroom." By nine o'clock that night the room was packed. With the beginning strains of the mellow music, the Frogges proudly led the first dancers onto the floor.

Chapter One

The foregoing is a brief description of the early history of Saint Joseph, Missouri borrowed from several sources. However, information describing his dream ballroom and the life of Frank A. Frogge's Frog Hop comes from a book written by Frogge's daughter, Birdie Heerlein. Published in 1984, the book's title is "Dancin' at the Frog Hop". It is a wonderfully descriptive, lovingly written, detailed documentary of her father's enlightened aggressiveness, force of personality and the realization of his dream. A reader of a certain age will marvel at the numbers of popular name bands who were booked repeatedly by this ballroom in the nineteen thirties, forties and into the fifties. As one who remembers with much fondness dancing at the Frog Hop before and after World War II, this writer will vouchsafe that Birdie's book is an historical gem.

* * * *

Everything written to this point in my story is absolutely true from my reading and recollection of fountains of information condensed in the foregoing description. But from here on, speculation takes over as the narrative includes a story line with which I, the author, take many liberties.

Among the celebrants at the Frog Hop that New Year's

Eve in 1928 were a man and wife who had driven a handsome new Buick sedan from their farm fourteen miles south of Saint Joseph. Phil and Sarah Eckner's fertile Missouri valley "bottom" land extended north and south on both sides of Highway 59 after it takes an abrupt swing west three miles south of the small town of Rushville. Their house and outbuildings were only two miles from the toll bridge that crossed the river to Atchison, Kansas. Phil Eckner (and Sarah) had inherited the farm two years earlier, apparently leaving no family members back east. and had worked hard to make the wheat farm profitable during the recent good crop years. Also, it became generally known that the Eckners commanded substantial resources beyond the more than a thousand acres of farmland.

Phil was a strapping six-footer with a classic face bronzed by the sun and a head topped with dark luxuriant hair. Clear blue eyes seemed to twinkle when he smiled displaying perfect white teeth. He was clearly outgoing and enjoyed the company of people of all social levels. His wife, Sarah, was slender, blond with big amber eyes and considered by all who knew her, to be very pretty. Both, then in their mid twenties having come to Missouri from the Northeastern United States, were pleased to learn they were obviously quickly accepted into the region. Phil and Sarah were athletic and seemed to have a passion for dancing to the growing popularity of swing music. Sarah had mentioned to friends that they often attended dances as far away as Kansas City, Missouri and Des Moines, Iowa when big name dance bands were performing. As news reached them of the construction of the gorgeous new ballroom in Saint Joe, they were ecstatic. When tickets were offered for sale, Phil quickly obtained some of the first available which were priced at a hefty dollar a couple.

As the United States greeted the nineteen thirties with a change in leadership in Washington, DC, the nation was reeling from the economic depression which began with the stock market crash in October. 1929. However, despite the outlook nationally, the Frog Hop Ballroom attracted crowds of young people who came to soak up the atmosphere created by the appearance of the Big Bands in that excellent dance hall. Tickets at the door in those difficult years generally cost 25 cents per person.

The repeal of the 18th Amendment in the early thirties signaled the end of prohibition. At the Frog Hop the house policy mandated that legal booze could now replace bootleg liquor(hidden in paper sacks or under a table)…but legal spirits were not yet sold inside the ballroom. However, "setups" of soda and flavored soft drinks were available. Of course, the Eckners were always circumspect when bringing their favorite beverages to the dances they attended almost every weekend.

In April of 1935, one noon- time when Phil pulled his planting rig into the drive he joined Sarah for their mid-day meal. After tossing his cap on the hall tree, smiled sideways and said, "You know Sweetie, that flat acreage across the highway could be turned into a swell runway for some kind of airplane." Washing up quickly, he turned still with an expectant smile to face his intelligent and always attractive wife.

Sarah paused, looking sideways at her husband while she placed utensils on the kitchen table. "What?"

"It just came to me. We've been driving the roads a lot for several years, Saint Joe, Kansas City, Des Moines, even up to Omaha for odds and ends. I've been thinking about taking flying lessons and maybe buying a little airplane. It could save a lot of time and, yeah, be fun. What do you think?"

Phil seated himself at the table and looked up expectantly at Sarah.

The couple's marriage of more than ten years had not produced any offspring, so each devoted more than the usual affection and attention to each other. People in the area who knew Phil and Sarah could sense that closeness which was evidenced during this conversation about Phil's idea of acquiring an airplane. Sarah smiled, touching his arm lightly, seated herself and said, "Let's do it. I just knew all those chats about flying with Charlie Brown would stir your interest in flying."

Charlie Brown owned a tank truck and called on the Eckners from time to time. He was also a well known aviator who spent considerable time flying; even building his own airplanes in a large brick structure in nearby Rushville. He held a patent on an airplane engine with two reciprocating propellers which increased power and reduced the torque that happened with conventional single propeller aircraft engines. Phil had already asked the pilot/inventor if he might give him lessons while flying one of his conventional two-place airplanes. Charlie Brown readily agreed. Actually he was delighted as most of the people in that part of the world at that time felt flying was literally for the birds.

It was subsequently agreed that Charlie would provide Phil with the requisite instruction in one of his recently constructed mono- wing aircraft. All the pilot asked was that Phil pay for the fuel consumed during the lessons. Both men agreed that there was ample space in the field across the highway that Phil had mentioned to Sarah, which could be graded down and planted with grass for the Eckner's own "airport." It was complete with a wind sock placed prominently at the east end of the created runway. Instruction took place once or twice a week that spring flying off a level field normally used by Charlie Brown west of Rushville. Meanwhile the new air strip was graded and grass seed planted so that by late summer it was ready to accept traffic. After one of the final lessons, and after Phil had passed all the flying tests required, the two men, with Phil at the controls, landed on the Eckner airfield. Afterward, Phil shook hands with the pilot who taxied back for his takeoff. Phil bolted across the highway, stripping off helmet and goggles, flushed with the thrill of accomplishment. Sarah who had been alerted by the sound of the airplane had seen the landing. They embraced warmly. "Beautiful landing Super Pilot" Sarah said with a broad, dazzling smile.

"Thanks hon…what a thrill. Fantastic! But you know" he said feigning modesty, "Charlie Brown's airplanes are pretty basic. You really just fly by the seat of your pants and watch for landmarks, also obstructions, like that new KVAK radio tower over toward the river. Stuff like that."

Sarah led the way into the house and handed Phil the mail that had earlier been deposited into their mailbox out by the highway. One of the items was a mailing with a postmark of Bradford, Pennsylvania. The return address revealed that the letter was sent by the Taylor Aircraft Company. Inside the envelope was information about the company's currently successful model, the Taylor J-2 Cub, a high wing monoplane. As he perused the contents he murmured to Sarah, "Charlie Brown said he had tipped off these folks. Sarah, I understand that it has all the very latest in what some pilots call 'avionics, which means it takes *some* of the guesswork out of flying."

He handed the letter to Sarah, walked to the kitchen for a drink of water and returned to where Sarah was reading the proposal in the letter "Is the price right Phil? You would know." His reply was an enthusiastic shake of his head

Chapter Two

"I'll just take a train out to Pennsylvania, Sarah. Hey, maybe we could both head out right after the harvest ends here and fly it back. What do you think?"

After a brief pause, Sarah gave Phil another hug and a kiss on the cheek. "You set the time and then I'll see about getting the transportation out to Pennsylvania." And just like that, it was settled.

That year, 1936, was a watershed year not only for the Eckners but for their beloved Frog Hop Ballroom as well. For that was the year that Frank Frogge chose to turn over the enterprise to Tom Archer, owner of a chain of ballrooms in the Midwest.

Frogge by then had lost Clarence, his friend and manager of the Hop from the beginning. Also, it was believed that the energetic entrepreneur had pretty much run out of steam. But name bands continued to be booked and Phil and Sarah could be counted among the attendees for most dances.

The mission on the train to Bradford, Pennsylvania was without incident that last week in September. Phil, new pilot's certificate in hand, found the Aircraft company location then a place to spend the night in Bradford. Early the next morning they paid a visit to see the airplane offered to the Eckners.

As with most designs being manufactured for civilian use at that time, the Cub boasted an enclosed two person, side by side cabin cockpit. In record time, once Phil took in the lines of the Taylor Cub and heard the engine revved up, he was sold. He was also glad to see a two-way radio antenna stretching from atop the cabin back to the tail.

That Taylor Cub was one of the first of the J-2 line to be so outfitted. Finally, the company representative asked Phil to climb into the cockpit to get the feel of the little aircraft on a trial flight, accompanied by one of the top people at the Aircraft Company. Afterward, he was ready to close the deal. It was decided that Phil with Sarah would fly the J-2 Cub back to Missouri, though they only possessed conventional road maps. The range of the craft, according to the man at the company, would vary depending on head or tail winds. His final advice was to "watch the weather and don't let the gas gage drop much below one-half. And remember the three Rs...*Roads, Rivers and Railroads!* Follow highways, but locate railroads first, they are more major direction oriented and reliable. Most sizable towns have airports these days so you can refuel along the way." One other cautionary piece of advice the company man gave, also appeared in the accompanying Taylor J-2 Cub papers. "Be aware that this aircraft will not perform properly above a ceiling of fifteen thousand feet, Our advice: better stay under ten where the air is not so thin. So keep an eye on the altimeter, the altitude gage"

Meanwhile Sarah had shopped for some snacks and carried coffee and water which she stowed behind the passenger's seat of the plane. Then she tied behind her neck the blond hair that framed her face and normally fell loose to her shoulders.

Finally, after accepting the bill of sale and ancillary papers, the couple were ready for the great adventure of flying back west to Missouri, literally over unknown territory. Sarah was somewhat apprehensive as this would be her very first flight in an airplane. But always a good sport, she gave a nervous smile leaned closer and kissed Phil on his right cheek.When the engine turned over and Phil had adjusted the throttle, they were ready to taxi out to the end of the company airport. With a "Happy Landings" shout over the noise of the engine, the company man waved them on the way. The take off was good. The new Continental engine purred as they climbed for altitude.

Phil kept his eyes on the horizon as he was taught by Charlie Brown. But the instrument panel attracted his attention from time to time. Though his experience in reading a turn and bank indicator was nil, the compass, clock, oil temperature and altimeter were familiar to him and all were to become invaluable during this cross-country flight. Prior to boarding the Cub, he had spent some time in the flight room getting important instruction in navigating across the country. So with a ruler and a basic student's protractor, Phil had placed a map of the United States on the counter and penciled a line from Bradford to his first check point which was the airport at Cleveland, Ohio. He also identified various towns and cities along his planned route that might accept the little plane if they should drift off course. Meanwhile, he hoped to maintain a course of 220 degrees on this first leg. Nicely airborne, and climbing he saw that the altitude gage reached seven thousand feet at which point he leveled off, glanced and grinned at Sarah, shouting "How do you like?"

Sarah had begun to relax, intrigued by the new feeling of enjoying the view from high above the ground. She yelled back, "This new machine might just catch on with folks, you know?" Phil laughed and returned to his watching the sky ahead but also took in the undulating mostly green forested hills below that began to transition into neat farms.

Having left Bradford a little before ten, Bradford time, he hoped to reach Cleveland by mid afternoon, and then about two hours out, he found it : beautiful twin rails of shining steel remarkably directly ahead. His map had revealed railroads when they occurred between major cities."Now if the weather holds" he murmured. "We can follow those babies right into Cleveland." They had been facing a head wind so their air speed was not excessive, but, he thought, we're still going almost twice as fast as our Buick.

Radio communication was also in its infancy in 1936. Certainly the use of radio to control air traffic was a primitive addition to newly manufactured general aviation machines. Though just nine years earlier Colonel Charles Lindbergh flew alone, non stop across the Atlantic Ocean to Paris, France without the aid of radio communication. Charlie Brown had briefed Phil on the important features of air to ground radio, though his own planes had none. So, right now, this was a case of learning on the job. Thus Phil and Sarah found the listed radio frequency to contact the controller at the Cleveland Airport to announce their arrival. Through the headphones Phil received permission to land and refuel. They would find it convenient to spend the night in that big city on Lake Erie. It was a good thing too, as Phil found he was exhausted from the stress he didn't feel until he had landed, paid for fuel and saw that the Cub was tied down and the wheels chalked.

After being directed to a well reputed hotel and a satisfying seafood dinner, the couple retired to their room. Following hot baths, they fell into bed and both began to relax. Sleep overtook them quickly.

The wake-up call came early…six o'clock. Phil literally leaped out of bed, strode to the window, opened wide the curtains to see the early sunlight casting long shadows along the street. In the distance Lake Erie shimmered as it reflected the faint sun's rays. "Weather looks good hon." With that pronouncement, the couple quickly dressed, then with bags in hand checked out of the hostel. Sarah made sure they were amply fortified with food at a nearby coffee shop that was open at that hour. After a short ride in a taxi cab the couple were deposited at the site of the Cleveland Airport.

They found the building that served as the airport manager's office and radio room where Phil acquired a new sectional map. After discussing the course he wished to fly on this leg of the flight, he also got the latest local weather forecast. At that point he laid out his proposed route which would be generally a compass heading of 320 degrees all the way to Saint Joseph, Missouri. The distance would be close to 450 air miles. Looking closely, comparing his road map with the sectional he could see that if he could maintain their planned course they would fly over Fort Wayne, Indiana and later, in Illinois, Peoria. Both cities should have airports for alternate landing locations if a need for fuel or emergencies occurred.

The prevailing winds were westerly so with the sun at their back Phil finished his check list and switched the ignition for engine run up, glanced at Sarah, grinned and said, "All set Babe?" Sarah smiled and nodded in the affirmative, secured the fiber seat belt and leaning forward placed a hand on the instrument panel casing. At the end of the east-west runway, Phil advanced the throttle and released the brakes allowing the little Taylor Cub the freedom it was straining to achieve. Again, the takeoff was routine. Climbing easily they found a smooth patch of air at eight thousand feet where Phil leveled off, glancing occasionally at the ground but maintaining a close attention to the horizon.

Though he couldn't tell for sure, the pilot began to feel the strengthening head wind was slowing their progress, verified by the air speed indicator. Additionally, on the horizon, he could see a layer of clouds that Charlie Brown, in his cram course on weather, recommended his student avoid at all costs. Sarah could see the billowing clouds ahead also and her resolve was challenged somewhat by seeing her husband's white knuckles and the sweat on his brow. "Phil, do we drop under that storm or rise above it?"

Before answering, his mind too was playing one option against the other. He had no way to judge the ceiling of the tallest thunder head and he knew the little Cub could find itself in an entirely unresponsive element. "We have a little time Sarah, let's look at the map! Okay, see that spire down there off to the right;.must be a church. Now look past me to the left. How long have we been in the air this morning?" Phil glanced at the clock and answered his question, two hours and, let's see, thirty five minutes." Computing his air speed and the time elapsed he assumed he was now flying over Indiana. Dropping down, yet maintaining the original compass heading, he began to examine the maps for less obscure land marks. When the smooth air was displaced by rough pockets, Phil chose to gradually nudge left rudder and pushed the control stick forward gradually. Leveling off at five thousand feet, he was relieved that his airplane remained below the gathering storm.With both heads swivelling left and right, eyes sweeping the still visible ground, it was Sarah pointing to the map and then off to her right where she thought she could identify a river that had a name, according to the map; "Phil, that has to be this river here" as she pointed to the map."Looks like the name is Maumee, something or other and it leads directly to that town you know about, Fort Wayne."

Phil dipped the nose again and cruised to only four thousand feet when he decided to follow their instincts and find an airport in the area. The clouds had by now obscured the sun and broad splashes of rain began to strike the windscreen. "Lets see if we can get a bit lower, Sarah. Try to spot any kind of air field." Again, Phil turned on his radio transmitter and called for anyone at the town ahead.

Sarah's river did, in fact, reach the city that had to be Fort Wayne, Phil thought. He spoke into the hand held microphone, "Fort Wayne Airfield, this is Taylor Cub on a cross country. Can you see us? We should be on your northeast quadrant. Would appreciate any directions you can offer as we require a place to land immediately." He ended his transmission with the sign now being used to end a call, "Taylor Cub, out"

Phil was thrilled to hear over the static in his ear phones, "We see you Taylor Cub. Make a left at two thousand feet and you ought to see our runways. Runway 27 is still open, come straight in." Sarah could not hear the voice on the ground but knew from her husband's expression that all seemed well. And, indeed the landing which included an extra bounce was successful. By now the rain was coming down in sheets with visibility almost zero. However, the voice in the ear phones directed the pilot to make a "one eighty" and taxi to the bright red building off the runway, which was barely visible. With the switch off, and the propeller at rest, a handler braved the rain and directed the two Eckners to the shelter of the airport building near a number of other aircraft.

Chapter Three

Much relieved, the couple exited the airplane while the ground handlers secured their Taylor Cub to the tarmac. Inside Phil smoothed moist hair out of his eyes and greeted the man behind the counter. "Nice day" he laughed, and reached over to shake the man's hand. Identification and information was exchanged before the Eckners could find a place to relax for at least the night. Who knew how long this delay en route would last. One of the men had retrieved their bags from the Cub, so they were directed to a nearby hotel and restaurant. It had been a grueling few hours and Phil thought, some lessons learned. Clouds that appear so benignly beautiful from ground level can be beastly aloft.

The Fort Wayne and northern Indiana area seemed to be well targeted by the storm that did not relent until late that night As a matter of fact, it continued to drizzle during and after breakfast. But as the young flyers reached the airport, the people there, including two other pilots, were optimistic that the worst of the storm has passed to the east and north. "How's it look to the west," Phil asked the airport man seemingly in charge. He responded not only to Phil but to the two other pilots awaiting clearance.

"Glad to say, Folks, telephone contacts report that the

weather is clearing and ceiling appears to be unlimited, at least all the way to the Illinois line." The airport spokesman continued, pointing to the Eckners, "Your Taylor Cub has been fueled and checked, so after you take care of expenses, you are good to go." Phil and Sarah exchanged glances and smiled and nodded a thank you, as the sun poked through a break in the residual clouds and reflected on the moisture-glossy surfaces of the Eckner's Cub.

Proficiency in any endeavor improves with practice or repetition of the task involved. Therefore, the skill of piloting his airplane improved with every flight. Phil was very much aware that he was far from attaining the exalted level of expert. Most importantly, he was accumulating confidence. After taking off from the Fort Wayne Airfield, the Taylor Cub was pointed on a heading that would take the Eckners directly over the town of Peoria, Illinois, thence on the same line to Saint Joseph, Missouri. On this leg of the journey, the weather was perfect...not a cloud visible anywhere. A rare tail wind following from the east aided in reducing fuel consumption, Phil recognized. So by the time they had sighted Peoria it was estimated they could reach Saint Joseph in less than two and a half hours ...and the fuel gage needle rested in the safe zone.

As they droned across the wide Mississippi River, Sarah sat upright to better take in the view at five thousand feet. "Oh look, Phil," she pointed to the river, "What a sight; how really wide. And look at the boats." Phil glanced at her and grinned.

Finally, after sweeping across the plains of Northern Missouri, they began to recognize landmarks that were easily identifiable even from that altitude. "Look," Phil said as they began their descent, "There's Highway 71", the busy north-south artery that bounded the city on the east. From that point all they needed to do was identify in the late afternoon sunlight, Highway 59 that would lead them to the "Eckner Airfield."

It had been a long day but with all conditions perfect, Phil "greased" the Taylor Cub onto the grass runway in a nearly perfect landing. Sarah heaved a big sigh, when the switch was turned off, unbuckled her belt and threw her arms around her husband."It's really good to be home!"

Phil had a fleeting thought that though the experience for him had been a lark, for Sarah, portions of the journey must have been tedious, though she never complained.

That evening over dinner the couple chattered on, alternately laughing, then turning serious as they recounted the landing in a driving rain storm at Fort Wayne. "First thing tomorrow," Phil said finally, I want to set up a log, Sarah, maybe you can help reconstruct the three days. I think I owe this information to Charlie Brown at least. And for our own record of the flight. Okay?" Sarah smiled and nodded yes.

In the days that followed, every morning Phil would gaze across the highway to see their Taylor Cub sitting out in the open, exposed to the elements. Since he was tending to farm business he hadn't taken the time to refuel and fly the plane. And fall was setting- in meaning that inclement weather could soon be the norm. On cue, there was the day Charlie Brown pulled in with his tank truck. A big grin presaged his greeting of, "Man, Phil that's some good lookin' bird over there. Where you gonna house it?"

After greeting his friend and mentor, Phil answered the question. "I've been thinking we will put up a little Cub-size hanger at one end of the runway."

Charlie suggested that he could erect a corrugated steel

building for a reasonable price…one that would keep the airplane dry and provide a depository for gasoline as well. Phil took his friend by the arm and guided him into the house. Over coffee, Phil and Sarah described to Charlie Brown the highlights of the cross country flight. Also, Sarah agreed that their airplane deserved to have a "house" of its own. Phil promised that he would deliver a more complete log of the flight in a day or two as the men walked across the highway where Charlie examined the Cub admiringly as Phil hosed fuel into the airplane's tank.

Before the end of October the Eckner's private hanger was erected. Painted on both sides of the Vee roof, was the slightly overstrained name, *Eckner Airfield*. During this time they enjoyed flying about over the immediate area, occasionally traveling up the river to Omaha to test Phil's expertise in landing and taking off at a large city airport.

However, their infatuation with dancing to swing music continued to motivate their attendance in the weeks following the flight from Pennsylvania. They rarely missed an opportunity to be on hand and enjoy the music of the well known Big Bands at their favorite ballroom, The Frog Hop. Quite remarkably, famous name bands such as Duke Ellington, Lawrence Welk, Kay Kyser, Harry James, Guy Lombardo, the wonderful Glenn Miller, and others performed to the adulation of the swing and instrumental enthusiasts in the Saint Joseph area. All these years the Eckners chose to drive a car the fourteen or so miles to Saint Joe. Of course, it was impossible to consider flying as at least half the round trip would be after dark, a time when all amateur pilots and not a few pros would ground themselves.

Chapter Four

After the change in ownership of the Frog Hop, Phil and Sarah became well acquainted with the new manager of the Hop, a charming, personable man named Jimmy Hakes who ran a clean, no nonsense house. As emphasis, he found it appropriate to hire two good sized bouncers to make sure order would be restored if too much imbibing caused a scuffle or aggressive behavior happened. Jimmy Hakes was also a good manager of the proceeds that the new owners especially appreciated. Before long, Jimmy recognized the Eckners whenever they came to the Frog Hop. Eventually he made sure that their preferred table be reserved, though early on, such reservations were not a policy generally. Their table was always against the wall on a slightly elevated tier located on the band's left. They believed that in that location they could efficiently reach the dance floor. When seated, they could absorb the appearance, sound, phrasing and skills of the musicians and vocal artists.

Throughout the years, 1937 and 1938, the close friendship of the Eckners with handsome Showman Jimmy Hakes and pretty, petite, dark haired Evy flourished. It was not unusual for the foursome to enjoy dinner together at one of the finer restaurants in the Saint Joseph area on nights when the Hop was not open. At dances, both Jimmy and Evy would be working at their various tasks making things move along smoothly paying only passing friendly attention to the Eckners. On two occasions, Phil took a delighted Jimmy Hakes on a flight in the Taylor Cub to Kansas City to have a good look at the Play More Ballroom. Since there was room for only one passenger both Sarah and Evy stayed home at the Eckners house.

November 13, 1938 was a gorgeous late autumn Saturday. Phil had re entered the house after dashing across the road to check on the Cub. Hurrying over to Sarah who had just emerged from the bath wearing only a towel. He snuggled his face against her perfumed neck and said, "Honey, I have a swell idea! Lets pop up to Omaha, have an exotic lunch, and shopping for gal stuff. We could easily be back home here before it gets dark. What do you say?" Sarah replied coyly, "Fine, do you agree that I might first get dressed?"

"It's your call Sweetie." A grinning Phil headed for the bathroom humming a popular tune. Sarah quickly donned her favorite form- fitting black slacks topped by a silk, ivory blouse.

Within the hour, Phil and Sarah had trotted across the highway to their airport for the spur of the spur of the moment flight. Phil once again routinely checked the oil level, performed a visual inspection of the prop, undercarriage, ailerons and rudder cable connectors. It was only about nine a.m. when Sarah squirmed her slim body and long legs away from Phil as he entered the cockpit from her side of the airplane. Take off was only minutes later.

Within less than a half hour, the Taylor Cub had carried the Eckners to a smooth landing at the Omaha Airport. Phil did as instructed and taxied to the east side of the main landing strips where other private aircraft were parked. They soon left the airport by taxi.

The airport cab transported Phil and Sarah to a favorite place to dine, the Blackstone Hotel dining room. After consuming an early brunch of Nebraska beef and a salad, they asked for the check and also requested that a taxi be called. The driver took them back east on Dodge Street to Brandeis Department Store where Sarah wished to stop for a few minutes. Forty minutes later, clutching a familiar store tote bag, Sarah took Phil's arm as they walked out to the sidewalk hoping to hail a cab.

Surprisingly, as they emerged from the store, they were aware that a cloud cover had obscured the sun. Sarah glanced at Phil with a questioning expression. Phil only pursed his lips and murmured, "A bit of a change, huh?" Short minutes later, a taxi stopped for them. Within another twenty minutes they were deposited at the office on the private aircraft side of the airport. They dashed into the building, and immediately settled up with the person behind the counter. Phil asked if the weather would permit him to take off. "So far, so good" the man answered."This system doesn't seem to have any rain with it right now. But watch the cross winds that sometimes occur this time of year.The couple hustled out the tarmac door and made ready to board their Taylor Cub lined up nearby. Winds began to blow in spurts as they walked to the Cub, bareheaded which allowed the strong breezes to whip Sarah's long blond hair into disarray.

As the couple were seated and strapped in place, Phil started the engine. He calledAirport Control for permission to taxi preparatory to take off. "Affirmative Taylor Cub," the voice answered. As Phil slowly moved the airplane to the main north-south runway, Airport Control broadcast a general alert, "Trans World flight reports severe near surface down drafts on landing and takeoffs." Phil acknowledged with a "Roger," then continued on a course that would take them to the end of the runway and reported he was ready. Control then gave him the go ahead. As Phil advanced the throttle the small craft shook from the vibration and the wind gusts outside. Soon they were hurtling down the concrete strip, It seemed to be a normal lift off as the Cub rose some ninety feet into the air when the airplane inexplicably suddenly nosed down, crashing the Cub and occupants to the ground.

Inside the cabin a suddenly dreadful, frightening scream came from Sarah which was the last sound a white faced Phil Eckner heard as he mouthed the words, "Oh God, oh no." In that last split second before black silence enveloped him he had an impression of intense heat.

* * * *

The *Omaha World Herald* and radio news reported on the tragic accident at the Omaha Airport. The reporting was straightforward, describing what was known of the crash. Authorities assumed that the Taylor Cub, while on a normal take off was stricken by a sudden violent down draft that effectively counteracted the normal lift characteristics aircraft depend on for flight. Sadly, the information disclosed in every story's lead, *that the young woman identified as Mrs. Sarah Eckner was killed. Her husband, Phil Eckner, the pilot. is in critical condition at an Omaha hospital.* The story gave Missouri as their home and not much more information. *The resultant fire was quickly contained by the fire fighters at the airport but not in time to save Mrs. Eckner who was only 35 years old.*

Word of the tragic accident spread rapidly through the Saint Joseph and Rushville area. Most of the Eckner's neighboring farmers were stunned at the news with the qualifying caveat expressed, 'who will tend the farm'. However, it was close friends such as Jimmy and Evy Hakes who paid a half dozen sorrowful visits to the hospital in Omaha. Charlie Brown knew better than anyone in the area the risks inherent flying fragile aircraft in those times. He was also convinced that from visual accounts, described in this case, that capricious winds can cause problems without rhyme nor reason, that the crash was not necessarily Phil's fault. Nonetheless, Charlie privately grieved. He managed to visit the hospital once in that early three -day period while final arrangements were made for Sarah Eckner who was interred after a brief service, in Ebenezer Cemetery on the south edge of Saint Joseph. Jimmy and Evy made these decisions after consultation with the Eckner's attorney and the Pastor of the Rushville Christian Church. A Saint Joseph lawyer became the focal point of other advice for the authorities. Only lawyer Sam Cowan and banks in Saint Joseph and Rushville knew anything at all of the resources commanded by t he Eckners. Charlie Brown, Jimmy and Evy Hakes were close friends but were never consulted or involved in the Eckner farm business or other endeavors.

The tragedy of the crash and subsequent events that followed, provided grist for the rumor mills in the area while Sarah was put to rest and a comatose Phil struggled to survive. Doctors agreed that it was most remarkable that the patient did not expire as his head suffered a great deal of trauma from the plane's collision with the ground and the resultant fire. Early on the fourth day, Phil Eckner regained consciousness, and for the first time learned about Sarah. While his face, eyes and forehead were swathed in bandages he expressed his grief by weeping and verbally flagellating himself for causing the accident. Twenty four hours later he seemed to withdraw into a cacoon, communicating with the medical staff and nurses in monosyllables. At one point during these days a Roman Catholic priest who happened to be in the hospital, came to Phil's bedside. There the cleric offered remarkable advice. He laid a hand on the patient's shoulder and in an almost enigmatic soliloquy in a sensitive voice, knowing the deep grief suffered by the patient spoke these words: "You know, Mister Eckner, the flesh is temporary, only a temple for the soul, precious and always an inextricable part of someone you love." With that he said a prayer and bowed out of the room. Phil absorbed that logic and thus began a quasi- positive response to his fractured world, accepting that preternaturally, he was alive.

Chapter Five

Five days later, when he learned that he lay in a hospital in Omaha, Nebraska, Phil expressed the wish that he be transferred during his rehabilitation to one of the hospitals in Saint Joseph. With Jimmy Hake's help the transfer was accomplished. As most folks acquainted with the Eckners knew, being in closer proximity with the patient would accommodate everyone. Thus, apparently, signs of Phil's miasma seemed to be vanishing.

Now that Phil was back in Missouri, he welcomed visitors as he was able to sit up. Though barely recognizable with his wounds obscured by bandages he could make small talk. Miraculously he retained blurred vision in one eye through, or around, the wrapping. the other eye at this point, was questionable. But when Sarah was even obliquely mentioned in conversation, he would break up. During the remaining days and weeks he was hospitalized Phil's moods were unsettled. One day when his friend Charlie Brown paid him a visit, Phil began to talk about crashing the Taylor Cub. Though part of his mouth and one eye was covered with taped bandage, he offered, "Charlie, it was my own idea to fly to Omaha. and Sarah was so excited." Then he sobbed and in a muffled voice croaked, "I never got to say 'good by' What have I done?"

Poor Charlie felt deep compassion but he knew he was ill prepared to offer much help, though he stood, took one of Phil's hands and said, "Phil, old buddy, what happened was a freak accident, don't beat yourself up. Sure a terrible tragedy happened, but Lord be praised, you are here and all your friends will help you recover in every way." That may have been the longest speech Charlie Brown had ever delivered on a subject other than piloting an airplane. As he released the patient's hand he headed for the door and waved as Phil articulated, "Sorry Charlie, Thanks."

As the majority of bumps, contusions and bruises Phil had acquired in the crash had sufficiently mended, he impatiently asked to be released. The bandages he discovered were hiding the attempt at repairing the facial disfigurement the tragedy had caused. Looking with his still blurred vision at himself in the mirror without the masking bandages caused him to cringe in disbelief. He began to feel that he might never be able to reveal himself to others in this present condition. Yet he knew realistically that he must try to get on with his life., but now, without the one person he had ever loved, his beautiful Sarah...

A visit to the hospital by Jimmy Hakes, on the day Phil Eckner would be released was well timed. Jimmy, always upbeat, suggested. "You have mountains of things to think about, but when you begin to sort things out, Evy and I hope you will come back to the Hop right away. We've got Stan Kenton coming to play a week from Saturday. You'll remember we talked about his outstanding brass section?" Phil slowly nodded.

In a quiet voice, Phil answered, "Right now Jimmy, I would appreciate it if you would check with the floor supervisor to see if I can get out of here this minute." As Jimmy headed for the hall, Phil added, would you also be able to take me home. We can talk on the way." As was the custom, after signing himself out, the patient was efficiently transported in a wheel chair by one of the hospital Nuns to the exit where Jimmy Hakes helped him into the Hakes' car. Fresh bandages adorned one side of his face, covering one eye and edged over nearly to his nose. One side of his upper lip and a section of the chin were bandaged.

Conversation during the drive south on Highway 59 was sparse. Though Jimmy did learn that a condition pursuant to Phil's release was that he have a nurse call on him at home every day to make sure all his facial problems could be properly treated. He was advised to wait a few weeks before resuming any farm work required, even though it was now early winter, a static time for most grain farmers in Missouri. Jimmy accompanied his friend entering the Eckner house. When it became clear that Phil needed some time alone after the tragedy and all that had happened recently in his life, Jimmy said his goodbys, they shook hands and he headed for his car. "I'll call you," he yelled over his shoulder as he left the house.

That day Phil spent his time reclining on the couch in the living room. Neighbors had already deposited food, including a nourishing, still warm soup that he consumed.

That first night back, alone in his own house, Phil felt a desolate aloneness. When he finally entered the bedroom he had shared with Sarah, he literally collapsed on the bed, his head bowed into his hands and murmured, "Sarah, Sarah, Sarah." Finally, still feeling weak, he reached out for Sarah's multicolored Afghan which he draped around his shoulders. Minutes later he unfolded himself reclining on Sarah's side of the bed. Phil breathed- in the familiar scent on her pillow, remarkably sedating him. There he slept unmoving the entire night, temporarily subverting his intense melancholy.

He was awakened by the sound of knocking on the back kitchen door. Rousing himself he grabbed a robe and padded to the door. It was a middle-age woman wearing a nurse's cap, cape and a smile. "Good morning Mr. Eckner, I am Mrs. Hainline, come to dress your injuries. May I ?" Phil opened the door and invited her inside."Sorry, I was in bed."

"No problem, sir. I shall not be long. Are you ready for me to tend to you?"

"Give me ten minutes maam, please?" The nurse smiled and took a chair there in the kitchen as Phil retreated to the bedroom and proceeded to get dressed.

Nurse Hainline seated Phil under the ceiling light of the kitchen, so that she could see the job before her. As she removed the tape and gauze, she did not evince any kind of reaction, though Phil half expected her to register some kind of emotional revulsion. "I think, Mr. Eckner that you will be glad to know that I am seeing something good here. Through all the surgical trauma and scars, I am seeing evidence of your hair coming back after being singed or burned off, whisker growth too, albeit, a little uneven but it's coming back.Tomorrow, perhaps I shall take scissors or possibly your razor and see if we can resume some kind of normal routine on this portion of your face. The alternative might be to simply let your whiskers grow to eventually hide some of the scars. It will be entirely up to you."

It was not the most earth shattering decision he had to make at this time, but Phil responded in a respectful manner, "Thank you Mrs. Hainline, I shall let you know tomorrow." With that, new dressings were applied and the nurse bid her patient goodby. The donations of food began to tempt him, so with coffee heated up and some cereal he was nearly ready to face the day.

The farmstead office occupied a corner room on the main floor of the house. All the accumulated mail collected by one of the neighbors was stacked neatly on one desk awaiting his attention. Phil was amazed as he stood there shaking his head. This was new to him.neighbors rushing to help a fellow neighbor in a difficult time. By ten o'clock he had organized the mail, determining priorities. He made a note to call lawyer Sam Cowan in Saint Joe, also inform his insurance company and to phone banker Hiner in Rushville. A little later the phone rang and Phil heard the genial voice of Jimmy Hakes in the receiver. "Hi friend Phil, how goes it today?"

Phil answered "Well, the nurse arrived early and I've had coffee, so I guess not so bad. How are you Jimmy? How's Evy?"

We're all fine, Phil. Just want to remind you, I plan to have you picked up next Saturday and delivered to the Frog Hop that night if you think you can make it. What say you.? Stan Kenton's band, you remember. But if this is too soon, just say the word and we'll see you up here later on."

Phil paused, looked out the window directing his gaze across the highway to the Eckner Airfield and its empty hanger. "I am sorely tempted good friend. Let's see how I feel in a couple of days. I know right now I am getting stronger. We'll see how Nurse Hainline feels about this tomorrow morning. We'll talk then, Okay."

"Good enough, Phil. Oh yes, are you planning on hiring a housekeeper? Evy reminded me to ask you." Phil thought, my God, what else? But he spoke with only a trace of bitterness into the phone, "Let's talk about it later, Jimmy. Thanks."

With the conversation ended, Phil leaned back in his

chair, swinging it around to catch his still blurred reflection in a wall mirror behind Sarah's desk. "Who is that image" ran his thought processes... head almost covered by bandages much like the pictures of Egyptian mummies he had studied at length in *National Geographic* magazines or some repulsive, Quasimodo character from fiction? He mused, "Dare I try to resume my life as before without Sarah? Is it too soon to revisit the scene of our emotional, romantic outings...without Sarah? But why shouldn't I? Conflicted with these ambivalent feelings, he once more descended into a state of depression. Again, he was visited by recent past phantoms of regret which lasted until another neighbor called at the front door, laden with apparently one more baked item. The lady was poised and showed no overt reaction to Phil's appearance. Genial body language and a pleasant "thank you" dismissed one more kindly, neighborly gesture.

Chapter Six

The next morning, more rested in mind and body, Phil Eckner was at the door the minute Nurse Hainline appeared. Again seated in the kitchen in the same position, the nurse provided a hand mirror so Phil could observe the procedure of dressing the face. The disfigurement was, of course, obvious. "How do you feel about a trim or shave, or do you want to grow a beard and mustache, Mr. Eckner?"

"Let's go with the beard Mrs. Hainline, at least until the area fully heals up. Incidentally, what do you and the doctors think about my going out in public in a week or two ? Of course for awhile we would need to keep the injured part of my face covered so that folks won't be repulsed" This last thought was accompanied with a helpless gesture with his hands.

"Mr. Eckner, we will come up with a way to protect your face, also we'll continue to cover one eye because of the swelling around it. But my goodness, don't worry."

Your doctors say you can resume mobility as long as you don't yet get involved in work that might create physical stress such as lifting and running."

"On Saturday next, perhaps we can come up with a way

to protect this side of my face so I might go out. I have an invitation to attend the Frog Hop, you understand?"

"Absolutely, sir." We'll devise the perfect protection. And my semi-professional opinion Mister Eckner, is that music heals. Just a suggestion." Shortly, the nurse left and Phil began to regain a more positive air. He phoned Jimmy Hakes to give him the optimistic assessment of the nurse and to confirm that come Saturday he would be glad to be on hand again at a Frog Hop dance. It was agreed that one of Jimmy's "facilitators", his euphemism for bouncer, will pick him up at the farm by eight pm on Saturday.

On the appointed day, Nurse Hainline was on hand, though it was a weekend, and provided Phil with the somewhat smaller, fitted covering for the right side of his face. As protection for the area around the eye she had devised a black eye patch held in place by an elastic string. Though his head was mostly devoid of hair, one could see the outline of the new growth there and on his upper lip. Phil gazed with minimal vision into the mirror which gave him back his face, while his mind was sneaking around behind it and remembering.

That day, the Saturday of the Stan Kenton dance at the Frog Hop, Phil paced nervously through the rooms of the house. Donning a jacket he strolled around the brown lawn outside. He didn't venture away to the outbuildings nor across the highway…not yet!

Precisely at eight, the big dark car appeared in the drive and the driver, Phil tried to recall his name…it was Polish, he thought. As the man came closer to the front door, he recognized Joey Palitz, tall, thick-set and well groomed, one of the Eckner's favorites. After warm greetings and expressed condolences by Joey, they departed the farm. Within a little more than a half hour later they were at the Frog Hop on Saint Joe's outer belt road. With more than a little apprehension, Phil entered the front door of the Frog Hop where he was met by Jimmy and Evy who warmly welcomed Phil with hugs.

"Evy led the way as she headed for the "Eckners table" residing vacant up near the wall on the top tier of tables, though the crowds were filling up the hall. The band was assembling and tuning their instruments as Phil took a seat. Jimmy quickly joined him to point out the nearest exit which was in that corner of the hall."Just so you know, Joey will be available if you tire and wish to leave at any time. Okay? It is so good to have you back, Phil." Settled back, with his good eye roving the panorama of the gorgeous dance pavilion, his memories flooded back and he began to sob silently. He regained his composure as Evy strode by and seated herself tentatively across f rom Phil. He effected the nearest almost hidden impression of a smile, then leaned over saying softly, "Evy, early on my good friend and airplane mentor, Charlie Brown said something to me shortly after the accident. As I recall, he had a name for the crash. He called it, correctly, I'm sure, 'a freak accident.'

"I'm sorry Evy, but it seems I am the freak

"Phil, don't you believe it. You are still the same warm hearted man Jimmy and I have known from the beginning. And handsome, too. We can't change history or events. But we can trust in God. We can, and often do adapt. Now, just listen to that sound. Is there better therapy than creative Big Band dance music? The strong brass section was making it difficult to converse. "We'll be around later." Evy continued her rounds.

Before the intermission, when Joey made one of his calls at the Eckners table, Phil nodded and the two of them walked quietly through the exit. "I'll call the Hakes', Joey. but be sure to tell them I was tired and needed to rest." Palitz gave an affirmative nod, and led the way to the car. The emotional trauma had been too much too soon, as Phil leaned back, closed his eyes, pensive, and rested the entire trip home. The next day, Phil phoned Jimmy and Evy to apologize for slipping away without notice. Of course they understood.

The holidays of Christmas and New Year at the end of 1938 brought dozens of greetings, invitations and phone calls to the Eckners house. Phil, meanwhile had hired an older lady to clean and cook part time. Judy Marsh was recommended by one of the Frog Hop regulars. Phil hired Judy after an interview that lasted no more than five minutes. She was willing to come in four days a week, on a trial basis. Nurse Hainline's visits became more infrequent as Phil's beard and mustache were beginning to show a stubble that to observers lessened the shock of first impressions. At least that was his mind set. A checkup by his Saint Joe doctor also verified the diagnosis the nurse had given. He had driven to the physician in his own car.Afterward, Phil murmured to the image reflected in the rear view mirror, "Now let's see if we can heal the psyche."

Since he was not quite ready to resume even a modest social interaction, Phil responded negatively to the invitations that season. Catching up on the accumulated correspondence continued to occupy much of his time. And, of course, his best friend, lover, partner and super secretary was enormously missed. Jimmy and Evy kept in touch but chose not to issue another special- night invitation. Thus, Phil always scanned the pages of the morning Saint Joe Gazette and evening News Press for notices of bands appearing at the Frog Hop Ballroom. Since he was confident with slowly improving vision, that he had regained most of his driving skills, he would choose his own time for his re-entry into the Frog Hop night life.

One Holiday visitor, Phil was delighted to see was Charlie Brown, who brought some candy made by his wife. They spent an hour buoying each other's spirits.

It was past the middle of the month of March before Phil summoned the courage to drive to Saint Joe in order to hear the music of the popular Glen Miller orchestra. He appeared unannounced, lightly bearded, with only the eye patch indicating at a distance the most obvious evidence of his injuries. Truly, the hair on his head was beginning to make an appearance though somewhat scant and lighter in color than before.

His attendance this time was noted by several of his many acquaintances, some of whom paused in their moving around the floor to smile and nod in his direction. Eventually Jimmy Hakes learned of his presence and quickly strode over to the "Eckners Table" where he and Phil embraced in a manly hug, "Hey, good friend, you are lookin' good," Jimmy said with a big grin.

"Thanks. Couldn't miss the Miller magic. Looks as if business is good," then both faced the bandstand as Tex Beneke gave his rendition of *Chattanooga Choo Choo*. Jimmy again shook hands and over his shoulder as he left said, "Evy will be delighted to see you. She has a friend she wants you to meet."

Phil, standing with his arm stretched in a wave as Jimmy departed, froze in the position momentarily. Then, slowly lowered his hand and seated himself. During the intermission, as the crowd began to return to their tables, Phil unobtrusively as possible, left the building, and drove home. Though he had no idea who Evy wanted him to meet, but if it were another woman, he would rather delay any such liaison, at least for now. He regretted slipping away without seeing the Hakes' but in a near panic, he chose to disappear from the scene that night. Paradoxically, Phil knew that viewing and listening to Frog Hop bands would hasten recovery.

No question, he thought, life can be complicated.

During the ensuing phone call the next day, Phil explained that his sudden departure was a result of his still prevalent self consciousness. As much as he liked the phrasing and style of the Miller band he said he felt uneasy. "So, I just quietly slipped out. Sorry Jimmy."

"Evy understands too. Though she describes you, lovingly, I might add, as some kind of abstract, specter (in the good sense)...she also uses the fanciful descriptive name, '*Phantom!*' Imagine that! Guess it's because 'now we see you up here and then we don't.' No one else but you know what you have been through and the loss you have suffered. I just want you to understand we are on your side during this period of your readjustment."

Phil replied that he appreciated their concern and again repeated his gratitude for their affection, help and advice since last November. Then in a magnanimous moment, he suggested that Jimmy tell Evy that in a few weeks he will return to the Hop and would, if the offer is still applicable, be pleased to meet the person to whom she referred last night.

The call ended on an amicable note.

Chapter Seven

It was April before Phil made another trek to the Frog Hop ballroom. Don Hoy, a band well known in the area, was playing, one that the Eckners always enjoyed. Having been alerted, Evy brought a guest to the table soon after the dance music began. She lead by her hand, a dark haired, very attractive woman who looked to be in her mid twenties "Phil Eckner, may I present my friend, Alice Bancroft. Allie, meet our good friend, Phil Eckner." Phil smiled and motioned the ladies to be seated as he repositioned two vacant chairs.

After helping to encourage conversation, Evy excused herself leaving Phil and Alice Bancroft alone sipping soft drinks. Brushing some errant hair away from her turquoise eyes, Alice offered the notion that she had known the Hakes' for several years. "Well, truly I have known Evy longer, we lived in the same neighborhood in Kansas City and went to the same school, though not in the same grade. For the past three months I have been working here in Saint Joe, at Quaker Oats."

Phil placed his drink on the table. "What do you do at Quaker Oats, Allie?"

"Oh, it's not much, but I am getting some experience in the marketing department; I'm two or three job levels below the department head. Evy tells me you are a farmer and a pilot."

"Well, Evy's half right. I guess you might say I am a farmer these days, period." He softened the expressed harsh thought with a smile. When the mellow beat of the popular tune, *In the Mood* sounded, Phil surprised himself by asking Alice if she would like to dance. She quickly agreed by saying, "I would love to."

For the first time in all those months past, Phil was on the dance floor, of course not with his beloved Sarah, but with a lovely young lady who also happened to be a good dancer. At least she followed his lead nicely.Afterward he followed Alice to the table where they remained seated while discussing the music, the Frog Hop and Old Saint Joseph. Halfway through the second half of the evening, Phil stood up, took Alice's hand, kissed it and said he would be leaving."Tell Evy that I have had a delightful evening and I will certainly be calling you, but I must go now. Evy and Jimmy will understand."With that he left a somewhat nonplused lady faintly waving to him as he left by the corner exit.

Phil had parked his car near the preferred exit to the Hop. Thus it was only a few steps to reach the means of this latest retreat. Breathing heavily, he took the steering wheel in both hands and rested his head lightly there. Joey Palitz was aware this time of Phil's quick exit and happened to see him motionless at the driver's position. As he approached the car, Phil looked up, rolled down the window and said, "I'm okay Joey, I am still easily tired and I'm taking off a little early." Palitz gave him a wave as Phil drove out of the parking lot and headed south toward home. He mused to himself "The Phantom strikes again. Damn."

Now, it was almost routine. Phil phoned the Hakes

residence the next morning and thanked Evy again for her thoughtfulness. He was just 'a bit fatigued' last night. "I really enjoyed meeting and chatting with Alice, and will call her before long. Thanks much, Evy."

During the planting season, Phil had hired some men to help with that extensive process. The housekeeper, Judy Marsh had voluntarily reduced her hours at the house, and Nurse Hainline no longer made daily visits. Phil was slowly feeling re-energized as the miracle of healing began to be asserted throughout his system. By the month of May, 1939 he was able to cast off the black eye patch, though vision in that eye was not perfect. The trimmed beard and mustache were distinguishing features on a face that began to resemble that of the former Phil Eckner. Later, on a glorious day that spring, he phoned Evy Hakes."Hi Evy, this is Phil. I don't have Alice's number, would you be so kind as to ask her to join me at the Hop Saturday night?"

"Well certainly, Phil. How are you these days? Dear one, are you managing your, what shall we call them?...demons, or whatever? Jimmy and I have been so concerned"

Phil was silent for a couple of beats then, "Evy, I will never be the same as before. My Sarah is the last thought I have at night and the first that enters my mind each morning. Call the condition what you will. But I am determined to rejoin humanity so you folks and your friend, Alice, will surely help, in fact have indeed helped. Okay? I'll see you all on Saturday if all goes well." With a positive response from Evy, they terminated the call.

That Saturday night the band turned out to be the talented organization led by Duke Ellington. For the first time in this new life, Phil felt more at ease during the evening. He and Alice danced several dances. It was only near the end of the performance that Phil once more felt the need to get away. But this time, the elusive "Phantom" was accompanied by Alice. She didn't mind leaving with Phil as it made her feel she might now be a part of his life, after all. He followed her directions and deposited her at the doorstep of her apartment on Mitchell Ave. He kissed her lightly on the lips and retreated to his car, and thence home to the farm.

At least once a month through that year and into the year 1940, the couple were together either at the Frog Hop or at a movie. The outing always included dining out. Occasionally they would find a corner table at Heinies, a favorite dine and dance juke-box bistro for the younger set located conveniently on the Belt Highway. Though they had very little in common other than the love of music and dancing, they managed to develop a friendship that for now did not include an intimate relationship. Both soon learned that there was that obvious age differential between them with Phil being ten years older than Alice.

The second anniversary of their meeting, was a reason for a small celebration at the Frog Hop. It had been two years since that day in March, 1939 when Phil was introduced to Alice Bancroft. It was now 1941 so Jimmy and Evy conspired with a number of friends acquainted with the couple to put together a party right there at the Eckner's table near the bandstand. It was a gala evening. For the first time in months, Phil began to relax. My, he thought, how long had it been since he had sampled a cocktail? The evening was crowned by the presentation of a dedicated number by the band to the couple.

That year, 1941, was a turbulent year. The news from abroad, mainly Europe, was not calculated to foster a feeling of stability. The German dictator, Adolf Hitler, was careering through Europe cowing the leaders of most of the neighboring countries with his threats and overtly with his military might. Only England which had found an indomitable leader in Winston Churchill was resisting valiantly across the Channel from German occupied Europe. America, at first covertly aided the English, later by means of a program termed the Lend Lease Act. The beleaguered island nation needed all the help it could summon.

Late summer that year Phil and Allie were seeing each other more often. Picnics at Lake Contrary on the southwest edge of Saint Joseph and outings south of Rushville at Bean Lake were relaxing times for Phil. But around the edges of his mind there prevailed memories of going through these routines with Sarah not that long ago. Of course, Phil had made regular pilgrimages to Sarah's grave in that Saint Joseph cemetery.

It was obvious that everyone especially Jimmy and Evy Hakes believed that Phil Eckner had found new love in the beauteous, charming person of Alice Bancroft. For a period of time Phil half shared that conclusion. Certainly, with every date he was more in tune with Allie…and it seemed obvious she cared deeply for him. So throughout that summer and autumn as the crops were harvested and he had more time to think about his future as he followed the headlines in the Gazette and News Press, The Atchison Daily Globe, occasionally, the Kansas City Star and Omaha World Herald for world news.

One Sunday, in late October Jimmy and Evy Hakes drove to the farm accompanied by Allie Bancroft. Phil had issued the invitation. On the phone the day before, he asked Jimmy if the three of them might join him in an old fashioned cookout. A neighbor had butchered a beef and had given some prime cuts to Phil. Jimmy said he would clear it with the girls, "but count on us to be there."

Evy and Allie set up a table in the house as Jimmy and Phil stood around the fire pit in the back yard. The topic of conversation was, of course, the war in Europe. Phil offered the opinion "Sooner or later we are going to be involved and I intend to be a part of it, if anyone will have me." Jimmy turned to face his friend, not as well informed as Phil, questioned, "Really? President Roosevelt has promised that he will not send American boys to fight in a foreign war." Phil turned the meat tilted his head up marveling at the sheep-like clouds scudding across the blue sky."All I know, Jim is that we can't sit by and let that maniac take over all of Europe. And who knows? Maybe the USA. With that he affectionately tapped Jimmy on the shoulder, with a grin, "but not until we demolish these nice, browned steaks." as Jimmy held open the door for Phil and the platter of beef.

Jimmy couldn't resist asking a little later, "How are you and Allie getting along? She seems to be carrying a pretty strong fancy for you mister farmer".

"She *is* a lovely girl. And I am very fond of her, but Jimmy, confidentially I have been blessed with only one love. And she is gone." Jimmy soberly nodded, already half suspecting an answer along those lines. But he thought, this isn't going to be easy when it comes time for Phil to bare his soul to Allie. Nothing more was said that day regarding the assumed romantic interaction between Phil and Allie. They continued to see each other and enjoyed a festive Thanksgiving at the Hakes home in Saint Joseph. A little more than a week later, on December 7, that year, the country was stunned to learn of the "Day that Will Live In Infamy," as Roosevelt described the Japanese sneak attack on Pearl Harbor, Hawaii. A day or two later Germany declared war on the United States.

Phil wasted no time in seeking to join the Army Air Corps. Though he was older than most of the candidates, he was after all, thirty eight. But with his already proven ability as a pilot, he felt he had a leg up, so to speak. Also, his eyesight had improved. Finally, after visiting the nearest Army Air Corps induction unit at Fort Leavenworth, Kansas he learned that he would be accepted with open arms and offered a commission. He would likely be assigned to an airfield where he could help train the huge flow of new cadets that would surely be entering the service. He would be sworn-in to the Army Air Corps on December 30. One of the first people he told was Charlie Brown who pounded him on the back and offered congratulations. "You'll do great Phil. Hang tough !

He therefore had time to arrange for his farm to be leased for the duration, plus closing up the house. It was not as simplistic informing his friends the Hakes' and Allie. But on Saturday, December 20th, at the Frog Hop Ballroom, seated as always around the Eckner's table, Phil made the following speech that he had rehearsed :

"Good friends and Allie dear one, a few days ago I volunteered to serve in the Army Air Corps. I don't know how long I will be gone, nor where I shall be stationed in this country or abroad. At first, I shall be training young cadets to fly. Now that I am healthy and also have a healthy respect for aircraft, I should be able to perform as required. My only regret is that I must, for now, say goodby and with a grateful heart thank you all for standing by the 'Phantom' these past few years." He and Evy embraced followed by a hug from Jimmy Hakes, who wiped his eyes and continued his rounds of the dance hall, followed by his Evy.

Then taking Allie's hand he said to her. "Sweet Allie, you have been a balm to my existence these past two years. You have been a major reason I have been able to resume some semblance of normalcy." He then hugged her and kissed her lips."Though we have never alluded to it, I have given private thoughts to asking you to be my wife. I do not know how you would have responded, but the fact is you are the best thing that has happened to me since my Sarah…" his voice broke as a tear glistened near one of Allie Bancroft's turquoise eyes. "However, there are too many ghosts and memories in my life to suggest that you consider waiting for me. Especially, since I shall be gone for who knows how long. You are precious and I hope, God willing, we will some day again find each other." Holding his hand Allie tenderly placed it against her cheek.

So Alice Bancroft maintained her poise at the end of Phil's farewell statement. She knew the times were tenuous and the entire planet seemed to be dissolving around her. But she showed her class in accepting one more embrace and kiss from that strange, complicated man, the "Phantom Of The Frog Hop," whom she would never forget.

Epilogue And Author's Note

All the elements of geography and topography in this novelette are accurate as is the description of the Frog Hop Ballroom. The account of the change of ownership in 1936 by a man named Tom Archer is true. Also, the Jimmy and Evy Hakes characters did exist though I have assigned them lives, if here today, they might not recognize. Charlie Brown was a real person and he is described exactly as he lived in those years. However, the main protagonists, Phil and Sarah Eckner are products of my imagination. .as is Phil's late nineteen thirties amorous friend Alice Bancroft, and the several other named persons. The Taylor Aircraft Company was actually located in Bradford, Pennsylvania having moved there prior to the year 1936.

Creating this Novelette, this work of fiction, made it possible to show again how devotion to the genre of music, and dancing to the legendary Big Bands could help heal body, and the soul, of one stricken by the sudden tragic loss of a beloved spouse, and accompanying disfiguring injury of the other. But more importantly the story reveals how innermost strengths of the survivor can emerge eventually, often long after the trauma occurs.

* * * *

NORTH ATLANTIC FLIGHT, 1944

Author's Prologue

The following is a composite of several experiences, accumulated from conversations and documents by various individuals I know, and with whom I served in the 351ˢᵗ Bomb Group, Eighth Air Force, during World War II. Beginning in April, 1943 this unit was based at an airfield near the hamlet of Polebrook in East Anglia, England.

All the names of crew members in this narrative are fictitious but the events described are very, very real as vouchsafed by those who were involved.

* * * *

Second Lieutenant Hank Weston, pilot and aircraft commander of the factory- new B-17, glanced downward to the North Atlantic. At this altitude of eight thousand feet, the sun sparkling off the wave caps in the leaden ocean gave a deceptive illusion of tranquility in the rosy after glow ribbons, of an early September sunset. Though the sky colors were behind them he was able to glimpse the display. Also, Hank was aware that from almost any altitude, a sea will not reveal the true degree of roughness that one finds at the moment of landing, or ditching, as the case may be.

They were less than an hour out of Goose Bay, Labrador, heading generally in an easterly direction. The task of

Weston's crew was to ferry this Flying Fortress, one of nine-teen others, halfway across the globe to a destination in the United Kingdom. The crew would later be assigned to a unit in the 8th Air Force for combat. All twenty B-17s were among the first produced that did not carry the dull green paint that imitated the fashion of the Royal Air Force. It was finally con-cluded that bombers flying missions at twenty five thousand feet, or higher, might tend to be less visible from afar showing only the natural silver color of the aluminum that enveloped the airframe.

Having achieved the recommended cruising altitude for this flight, Hank unlocked the throttle controls, nudged the levers back a bit, reducing the air speed to 145 indicated, lean-ing the mixture controls accordingly. As his eyes focused on the fuel gages, Hank Weston reflected on the circumstances leading to the assumption of total responsibility for nine other fellow crew mates and a flying machine that cost the taxpay-ers of the United States a quarter of a million dollars. He was twenty one years old! His home was Omaha, Nebraska and had attended the University of Omaha. After one year there he enlisted in the Army Air Corps flying cadet program.

Hank's parents were, as with thousands of others in Amer-ica, patriotic and pleased their son chose to enlist and serve in the "glamorous" Air Corps. His dad was a foreman at the Swift Packing Company and his mother worked as book-keeper in her new job at an Omaha hotel. He had one sister. two years younger. Physically, Hank was almost six feet tall and tipped the scales at a robust hundred and eighty pounds. One would also be impressed by his striking blue eyes and commanding demeanor. Apparently these physical attributes helped cast the pilot naturally into a leadership role as pilot of a four engine aircraft. Certainly, the men on this crew assumed an easy, yet genuinely respectful, admiration for Henry Weston, their aircraft commander.

In the Army Air Corps of 1943 a newly commissioned Second Lieutenant, having won the silver wings of a pilot was indeed fortunate, given the completion of the various training assignments, if he were listed to fly in combat the airplane of his choice. Weston was lucky. He had applied for and eventually received the news that he would transition into his first choice, the B-17, the most the well known Heavy Bomber in America's arsenal. He knew that this already famous aircraft was designed, and most were built, by the Boeing Company of Seattle, Washington. Hank had read that the prototype version first flew back in 1935. This particular plane today, carried the latest of many improvements, and was categorized as the Model G, boasting the distinctive maneuverable nose gun turret. Though the American 8th Air Force has been operational in the European Theater for less than a year, already it was widely appreciated that the four engine heavy B-17 bomber has been extremely successful in carrying the war to the enemy in Europe.

Continuing his musing, Hank remembered that it was late March this year, 1944, when he was ordered to Dyersburg, Tennessee where he would meet the other men who would serve as his crew members. There in Dyersburg the Weston crew would train, honing their skills for the combat missions that would follow after an intensive three month stretch of flying simulated missions.

All the crews of that training cycle at Dyersburg Army Air Base assembled in a barn-like hall barren of furnishing save for dozens of folding chairs placed in rows of ten. On the back rest of each chair was a card directing the ten members of the crew to take the chair assigned to his place on the crew.

Also stenciled was the news that his crew would be named "Crew 4144." On one aisle was the first chair that was designated for the pilot. Eager to attach a face to the names on the orders that he received only the day before, Hank was in place well before the appointed hour as aircraft commander of crew 4144.

His reminiscing was interrupted by a voice on the intercom.

"Navigator to pilot, over."

"Go ahead navigator, over."

"Navigator again. Suggest you adjust heading two degrees north to 093. Over."

"Thanks George. Out."

The pilot over road the automatic pilot, fingering the wheel on the control column just enough to bring the compass needle to the new course. Then he tapped the co-pilot's leg, gesturing that it was his airplane, and shouting over the roar of the four engines, "that second cup of coffee. Be back in a sec, Hop."

Weston unbuckled his seat harness and parachute and eased past the flight engineer. He made his way squeezing through the narrow opening to the bomb bay and equally scant walkway across the empty bomb bay compartment and stepped into the radio room immediately aft of the bomb bay. The man sitting at a small table that held the short wave radio receiver and near the edge of the table, a telegraph key, looked up and grinned as the pilot stood over him. Hank raised his voice, "Everything okay, Luke?"

Receiving an affirmative nod, the pilot grinned back showing the recognizable tiny space between his two upper front incisors. He stepped through the opening to the rear in search of the emergency device called the 'relief tube'.

Lucas Brooking Lewis glanced back, noting quickly that the four gunners were discreetly looking away as their aircraft commander urinated into the funnel-like appliance at one end of the hose. As the pilot re entered the radio room, the aircraft was buffeted by an unseen air disturbance. Hank used the radio operator's shoulder to maintain his balance. Shaking his head, and grinning big again he stepped onto the tiny catwalk leading through the bomb bay on his way to the cockpit, closing the small metal door behind him.

Crouching a little he made his way back to his seat and buckled up. He gave the OK sign to Jordan Hopper, the copilot who was also a second lieutenant. Running his eyes over the instrument panel Hank confirmed that all was well. His ears had already revealed that the four power plants were performing normally. Re establishing the auto pilot as he regained control from Hopper, Hank Weston had time to think about his crew. He had previously assessed their performance in Dyersburg. But he had, in the process, garnered bits and pieces of personal information about all the other members of this crew under his command.

For example, he knew that Jordan Hopper was from Mississippi. Hattiesburg claimed him as a lifelong resident growing up in the countryside of that important city. His father, apparently, was a tenant or 'share cropper' as Hop described their existence. His father continued to work the land, mostly cotton, but his mother died well before he joined the Air Corps. Hop was only a few months older than Weston, though smaller in stature. He rarely smiled, Hank noticed, and though very reliable, he sometimes conveyed a listlessness. But not on the job! The pilot was, indeed, glad to have him on board and beside him in the cockpit.

Darkness was approaching, almost obscuring the North

Atlantic. So, it was at such times aloft when Hank Weston's thoughts turned to his navigator, another second Lieutenant, George L. Ohlen. Ohlen was seated lower in the nose and just ahead of the flight deck. His maps and navigation aids within reach at the minuscule table on the left side of the plexiglass enclosure. Hank smiled with amusement when he recalled that, for some unknown reason George made certain that everyone he met was informed that the L. in his name was important, "L is for Leander." The big blond twenty-year-old was from Ely, Minnesota and was intensely proud of his Swedish ancestry...as when he would bandy words with the others he would refer to himself as the 'Swede.' His competence as a navigator is being tested, the pilot knew on this Atlantic crossing.

Also normally stationed in the nose is the bombardier. His name is Bracken Davids. He claims San Francisco as his home, is married and at twenty five is the most senior in age of the officers in the crew. Those facts, Weston admitted, amount to the sum total of what he knew about his bombardier. His rank was flight officer, not quite commissioned, and certainly not enlisted. Flight officers were, however, privileged to wear the same nifty uniform of the commissioned officers. Bracken, as the most fastidious member of the crew, always looked well turned out. Hank did know that his bombardier received good grades in his specialty with the Norden bomb sight at Dyersburg and did passably well in gunnery, though he had not yet fired the twin fifties in the new nose turret that was added on all B-17 G models.

The fifth crew member forward of the bomb bay is, in the opinion of Hank Weston and most of the others, the most colorful and delightful guy to have around. He is the staff sergeant and crew chief, engineer, top turret gunner, a Mexican-Dane whose legal name was Haysus Andersen. He hailed from the Red River valley area of Oklahoma. Early on, in an off duty colloquy with him, Weston learned that the spelling of Haysus was a compromise his Mexican mother made with his Danish father. Apparently, his dad could not abide his son carrying the name Jesus (and spelled accordingly). In his Roman Catholic dad's parochial opinion it would be sacrilegious to have a mortal offspring carry the same name as Our Savior So baby Jesus became baby Haysus with the phonetic spelling in English.

Hank stole a look back and up, taking in the swarthy profile of his crew chief at his position behind the pilots, staring intently at the aircraft instrument panel. Continuing to reminisce, the pilot chuckled to himself remembering his crew chief approaching the aircraft and crew on the hard stand at Goose Bay earlier today saying in his trademark Okie drawl, "You all never fear, Jesus is here." Of course, he used the Anglo pronunciation. which lightened the mood of the others. At twenty six, Haysus was older than the other enlisted men and more prepared for his job, having been in the Army Air Corps since he enlisted at nineteen. He was a staff sergeant. It was most apparent that both Weston and Hopper were happy to have Haysus looking over their shoulders calling out airspeed when landing and other data the pilots requested. Hank also got a kick out of the time Haysus threatened to sever the tow line pulling the target on a low level gunnery mission in Dyersburg. In fact, from the top turret that very day he opened fire with the twin fifty caliber machine guns and the target fell away, of course to the cheers of all the gunners.

Cracking over the intercom, the pilot heard a Minnesota accent, "Navigator to radio, over."

"This is radio, go ahead, over"

"This is navigator. Luke, could you get me that QDM, if you can raise anyone?"

"Roger, wilco. Out."

Most members of a bomber crew were somewhat familiar with the 'Q signal' QDM that radio operators utilized to aid navigators in seeking or verifying position and or direction. It was quite simple in concept, and an exercise that most radio operators memorized and practiced in flight training. Basically, it amounted to the radio operator raising surface stations who could identify the plane's position by the expedient of using the depressed short wave key initiated by the radio man's transmitter on a pre arranged frequency, and by triangulation, respond with a determinate reading addressed to the call letters of the aircraft. Over the North Atlantic, however, securing an answer from radio range stations would be difficult if not impossible.

Henry Weston had heard all this before and knew that his radio man and navigator often these past months worked closely in defining direction and position. His thoughts turned to the man on his crew with whom he quietly felt a kind of kinship. Luke Brooking Lewis was also twenty one. Both Hank and Luke are products of Midwest upbringing as Luke came from a small town in northwest Missouri only about 150 miles from Weston's home in Omaha. Luke, however, was slightly taller of the two but more slender. His hair coloring and eyes are brown while Hank's short cropped hair is quite fair and his face, clean shaven. Luke shaved around a small mustache. Both families were Methodists. The senior Lewis was a country doctor while his mother maintained the records in the family's large two story home. There were also an older brother and sister. Luke being apportioned the arguable distinction of being the "baby of the family."

Luke Lewis considered himself fortunate in being assigned to a compatible bomber crew. He was a product of the ground forces, having been drafted and assigned to an Army base where he received intense conditioning. Learning that the Army Air Corps was recruiting other army personnel to transfer into the Flying Cadet Program, Luke eagerly applied, took the tests and passed handily. Near the end of the thirteen week basic training cycle he received his orders to transport himself to an air base in Texas. His time in the Cadets was abbreviated due to a serious mishap while piloting a trainer. He wrecked it badly on an attempted landing. He injured himself though not seriously. However, in the hospital he learned from a vindictive instructor the harsh news that he had washed out of the program. Even more extraordinary, he was skipped over for navigation or bombardier training... washing directly to one of the tech schools. In Luke's case, it would be radio school located at Sioux Falls Army Air Base in Sioux Falls, South Dakota.

So after six months, he had become an accredited radio operator. Six weeks of gunnery training in Arizona ensued after which he had crew member wings and a corporal's stripes. Very soon he received his appointment to the Henry Weston B-17 crew. He was directed to ship out to Dyersburg, Tennessee as a sergeant where he would meet the rest of his new crew.

Henry Weston was aware of Luke's military history and during an after hours break offered sincere commiseration to his radio operator. Hank, at their first meeting there in Dyersburg, recalled a humorous faux pas. When the radio operator approached 2nd Lieutenant Henry Weston, Hank shook hands and asked his name. Luke responded, "Lewis sir."

Hank repeated, "Lewisir, and your first name?"

Lewis hesitated a moment then explained. "Sir, my name is Luke Lewis." At that, Hank remembered, both men laughed. as he put his trigger finger to the side of his head afterward.

The pilot's thoughts were interrupted with the voice on the intercom.

"Navigator, this is radio, over."

"Go ahead radio, over."

"Had to use the trailing wire antennae but I do have a faint signal from bases in Greenland, I think, with our position." Luke spelled out the information for Ohlen. "Hope this helps. Navigator, this is radio, out."

"Radio, this is Navigator. We're okay. Your QDM is a roger that we have a good heading for Valley, with Meeks Field in Iceland providing an on course option if required. Thanks Radio. Navigator out."

Hank had suggested to all crew members that they man their stations on this flight. He thought of the cramped position suffered by Billy O'Mally in the ball turret and felt a twang of pity for him. But he had directed that, for most of the crossing, the gunners should be at their posts, just in case. Billy possessed the rare feeling of confidence and daring to be at home in the ball. He also had a pervasive sense of humor and was an accomplished story teller. O'Mally was from a small town in Eastern Kansas. Shortly after Luke had reeled in the trailing wire antennae, Billy emerged from the ball and ambled into the radio room. A grin was visible in the faint light from the radio operator's desk lamp illuminating also the ball turret gunner's copious freckles. He waved to Luke, yawned and lighted a cigarette and leaned back against a bulkhead.

Billy took a drag on the cigarette and looked directly at Luke. "We ought to tell Hank that I just noticed in the moonlight, some moisture seeping off the port wing. Just now it looked similar to a fog-like spray."

"Obviously, it couldn't be rain", Luke offered.

"Nah, it's clear as a bell out there, and with the moon, stars and all."

The radio operator sat erect, switched to intercom again, "Radio to pilot, over."Then squinting out the tiny window to his left he tried to make out the wing but it was impossible to focus on anything akin to moisture.

"This is the pilot, go ahead Luke."

"Hank, Billy just came into the radio room to stretch and reports that their looks to be a fog-like moisture coming off the left wing. It may not be anything important but thought you ought to know We don't have the altitude to create a freak contrail, do we? Radio, over."

For a long moment there was silence. Then in a controlled voice, Henry Weston spoke:

"Pilot to crew, we may have a problem. Our left fuel pressure gauge does indicate we may have an errant leak. Luke, tell Billy to put out that cig I know he just fired up, and get back into his ball and on the intercom. He's got to track that wing while he has some clear moonlight" Weston knew that Billy O'Mally was an inveterate smoker and would light up at every opportunity."Haysus will be directing a flash light from the top turret along the surface of the wing from time to time to try to add some definition for Billy. Will keep you all posted, out."

On the flight deck both pilots focused, their attention upon the fuel gauges.

They were very much aware that the new 'Tokyo tanks' tucked into nine small containers added between the outboard wing trusses on each wing were added to the G-Model

B-17s. They were so named on the theory that they would give the bomber range enough to reach Tokyo and return to a US installation in the Pacific. Hank knew that the point of departure would have to be from a base not terribly far from Tokyo. Or, in their present situation, he hoped to avoid adverse weather that would use up precious fuel.

Weston had issued few instructions to the gunners, all corporals, regarding their responsibilities on this cross-ocean ferrying mission…only to stay near their guns 'just in case'. The two waist gunners, Howell and Fregasso, and the tail gunner Shorty Stankowski were just now, all three, huddled aft of the radio room. Shorty had earlier crawled out of the tail on his hands and knees and was now preparing to return to his isolated position. …

On the flight deck the pilots and Haysus stared transfixed at the fuel gauges.

"Plenty of pressure on the right one, "Hopper offered.

Weston raised his gaze toward what had been a well defined horizon. Now it was black

"Engineer to pilot, over."

"Go ahead, Haysus. Can you make out anything?"

"'Fraid so Hank…the damn fuel cap over number two must be loose and the tank cover unclasped. Gas is siphoning out and spraying like a cow peeing on a flat rock."

"Haysus, I'm gonna need you down here, NOW!"

Then, "pilot to ball, anything new? Over."

"This is ball turret. Naw, it's too dark."

"Billy, you might as well join the gunners in the waist or radio room. Out. Shorty too."

Suddenly, chatter on the intercom ceased as each man aboard pondered the apparent options based on the limited information overheard. Radio operators on over-the-ocean flights were instructed to monitor 500 kilocycles, the international distress frequency, for a minute or two periodically. As Luke listened he hoped that *he* would not be one sending an SOS should this airplane began to settle onto the North Atlantic. He immediately subordinated that depressing thought. "We'll make it," he murmured, "Hank Weston knows his business."

Forward on the flight deck the pilot's mind was feverishly calculating the possibilities based on his reading of the fuel quantity and pressure gages. He was vaguely aware that his systemic boost of adrenalin sharpened his mind, realizing that he and nine other young crew mates were totally dependant on the skills of Henry David Weston. "God!" He mused just above a whisper, "Just fifteen months ago I was home in Omaha living an insignificant life as a Freshman in college. Now here I am not even old enough to vote, facing the first life or death crisis of my life. And I am not yet in combat!"

The return of Haysus to his position upright behind the pilot's seats, placing his hands on the seat backs, interrupted Hank's ruminating.

He turned and pulled the engineer close so he could talk into his ear. "Listen carefully As you can read from the gages there, the port side fuel pressure is showing one hell of drop and the quantity gage is down as well. Here's what I want you to do When Jordan gives you the signal, we'll ask you to manipulate the fuel transfer and fuel pump switches. We ran through this back in Dyersburg. Do you remember?" Hank gripped his engineer's arm for emphasis.

Haysus nodded in the affirmative.

"First we want to run all four engines as long as possible on the number two tank to use up as much of the gas left there and conserving the fuel in all the other tanks. Okay?"

Again, Haysus gave a serious nod.

"Hop, whenever you're ready," Weston yelled over the roaring engines to the co-pilot.

Turning half around as far as his seat harness would allow, Jordan Hopner shouted at

Haysus, "Turn everything to number two…pumps and all…Now!"

Haysus turned the dials and activated the transfer pump switches expertly, then leaned back toward the pilots and made a circle with his thumb and forefinger signifying that the transfer was made as ordered. All four engines didn't miss a stroke as the hungry Wright Cyclone power plants droned on sonorously.

"Stay right here," Hank shouted. We may get another hour out of that tank before we do the next transfer. Hop, we probably oughta lean out the mixture and reduce the indicated to 130."

The co-pilot agreed with a grim nod, adjusting the mixture levers increasing slightly the turbo charged air into the fuel flow. Hank simultaneously edged back the throttles.

Weston again gave up the control column to the co-pilot and withdrew from his flight coveralls a copy of the orders given to him in Kearney Nebraska. He directed a flashlight on the pages and re-read the first paragraph of Operations Order #214 the usual Secret Classification noted, that he re-read as follows:

The following named crew WP by air to the aircraft indicated at the proper time from Presque Isle Army Airfield Maine via Goose Bay, Lab, thence the NORTH ATLANTIC to the European Theater Of Operations, London, England reporting on arrival thereat to the 8th Air Force Service Command, ATC Terminals and duty with the 8th Air Force. Alternate landing site en route, should conditions warrant, is Meeks Field, Reykjavik, Iceland.

Appended, were the names of Weston and the nine other crew member's names with their ranks and serial numbers.

Also noted in the orders, was the serial number of this new B-17. The first number of the six digits identifying the aircraft was the number four, thus verifying to Hank that this bright, shiny aluminum-silver Flying Fortress was indeed new, having been built recently, in fact, late in this very year, 1944. He knew that the first number of every B-17 serial number indicated the year it was built. In Army Air Force nomenclature, the first three numbers of the year in such cases were omitted from being included in the identifying number. Hank also knew the landing area in the United Kingdom would be an airfield at Valley Wales, should they be fortunate in making land fall in the UK…

Taking his eyes off the printed orders, Hank smiled grimly thinking privately that he now knew why the army clerk who cut these orders chose to capitalize 'North Atlantic Route.' He recalled that they had followed the briefings back in Kearney, Nebraska. From Kearney they had proceeded East, landing at Syracuse, New York. After an overnight there they took off for Presque Isle for another over night respite before departing toward their final jumping off station at Goose Bay, Labrador. Goose Bay turned out to be a tiny speck in the wilderness where the United States Army Air Force operated a convenient last impression of land, including a landing strip, before the crews set out for the European Continent. Once the base was located, Hank was forced to use all his skills in trimming and settling the B-17 onto the runway that had been carved out of the landscape A fond recollection, however, was the wonderful Finnish sauna that all enjoyed that evening before departure time the next day after the fuel tanks were topped off with a total of 2780 gallons of gasoline...540 in the Tokyo tanks alone.

The pilot knew that, in theory, this should provide thirteen hours of flight aloft. Flying this route, riding prevailing west winds, in good weather would take eleven or twelve hours to reach Valley, Wales...thus, there was a comfortable cushion it seemed. But everyone on Weston's crew had heard rumors, some true, telling of military aircraft being ferried on these flights getting lost, apparently ditching in the ocean, never to be heard from. On this particular flight there was not a single sighting by Weston's crew of the other nineteen B-17s since departing Goose Bay and presumably taking a similar route to the United Kingdom.

The pilot also knew that departing Goose Bay at 2000 hours local time on this third day of September, they should arrive in Wales no later than 0900 the next day, British double daylight summer time. So, there should be ample daylight in that country that lies a little farther north than the province of Labrador in Canada. In September, the daylight hours recede with deliberate slowness in the northern latitudes.

"Navigator to Pilot." Ohlen's shout penetrated Weston's thoughts. "Hey, the stars are gone. Where did those freaking clouds come from?"

"George, how long has it been since you shot the stars?"

"Too long Hank. Can we get out of this mess? Positive we are okay but need a new fix."

"Navigator, this is Pilot. Lets hold this course for awhile. The weather briefing officer in Goose Bay said it looked good all the way across, You remember! This has to be a minor aberration in his forecast. Over."

"If this is the leading edge of a full grown frontal storm," the Navigator replied through gritted teeth, "I'll personally look up that little knothead and kick his aberrant butt from Hell to breakfast."

"Relax George L." Hank had to smile.

Back in the radio room Luke also gave a nervous chuckle at the exchange on the intercom. Colorful language is clearly part of the lexicon of most soldiers and can be helpful in conveying a simple thought. Some men in uniform, as with Haysus and Billy, straight forward cussing was endemic.

Usually, George L. Ohlen would find an acceptable Anglo Saxon drawing room expression in lieu of a profane phrase. Obviously Ohlen was more than a little agitated about the loss of one of his usually reliable navigation tools, his celestial sextant. Luke and everyone else knew there were no landmarks on the Atlantic to aid dead reckoning navigation.

As Luke continued to monitor and log the various frequencies, all four gunners trooped into the radio room and seated themselves on the floor. Gordon Howell the left waist gunner and Donald Fregasso, who manned the other waist, seemed more bored than concerned. Eddie Stankowski yelled at Luke, "What's goin' on? "

O'Mally, in mock seriousness, and always primed to tweak a favorite target,.even in a perceived emergency, "Right now Shorty, we're lookin' for some road signs and a gas station." Then, Billy pulled out an Old Gold and flicked his lighter aflame, as Shorty gave him an elbow in the ribs. The tip of the cigarette glowed in the dim light of the compartment emanating from Luke's small table lamp. Luke knew the gunners would soon retire to their positions in order to find places to plug-in their new heated suits. The temperature at this comparatively low altitude would nevertheless be near freezing.

Luke tried to make out the facial features of the young

men…kids, really, with whom he would share experiences in combat. The waist gunners became close friends in Dyersburg and were presently huddled together. They shared upper and lower bunks during training which helped to cement their comradeship. Fregasso, a native of San Francisco, the son of Italian immigrants was about nineteen. Gordon Howell, left waist gunner was a little older, Luke thought about twenty two. He was from Mount Pleasant, Pennsylvania.

Eddie (Shorty) Stankowski, the tail gunner was the youngest member of the Weston crew at barely nineteen. He managed to stretch to a height of a robust five feet, nine. He was born and raised in Cairo, Illinois, one of four sons of a coal miner.

After several minutes Luke unstrapped himself from his chair, stood and stretched. He had just entered the time in his log, having written 0415, GMT (Greenwich Mean Time.) This meant, he knew, since the 8pm, (2000 GMT) departure, this flight should be approximately halfway to the United Kingdom by now.

When Luke sat again, re buckled his seat belt, over the intercom into his headset came the pilot's voice. "This is the pilot. It's still overcast so I have decided to test the thickness of this mess outside so George can get a decent bearing. Let's ease her up Hopper."

Knowing full well that increased rpms to gain altitude would devour more fuel, Hank had concluded that their odds were more in favor of knowing their position and *maybe* running out of gas. He knew it was a better option than being ignorant of their exact location and ultimately plunging into the sea below.

As the roar of the engines intensified and a climbing attitude was evident, crew members squatting in the radio room stirred nervously and began to shuffle back to their positions aft. Up front on the flight deck Hank activated the landing lights though he knew they could not penetrate the black void that was totally without definition. Within minutes there was rain pelting the windshield. The pilot automatically flipped on the windshield wiper switch while the aircraft continued a gradual climb. The wipers were ineffective given the speed of the aircraft, so Hank a trifle sheepishly, turned them off.

Haysus crouched tensely behind the pilots, leaning on each chair back as all three men concentrated on the instruments. It was Haysus who first noticed the rain had become snow as the altimeter needle moved perceptive past 9500 feet. He poked Hank's shoulder and pointed to an accumulation of ice on the wiper arms.

Hank's response was barely a negative nod as he compressed his lips. Then, securing the loosely hanging rubber oxygen mask to his face, the pilot switched again to the intercom channel, "Pilot to crew, we're going through 10,000 feet. Put on your oxygen masks. Make sure they are plugged-in and working. Report back to me starting with Tail. over."

"This is Tail. Mask on and workin'."

Every crew member reported in that oxygen was flowing into properly affixed masks, as the B-17 climbed steadily, buffeted relentlessly by the storm around them. Hank Weston activated the deicer switches with his left hand as the first ice spun off the propellers and clanked against the fuselage.

Co-Pilot Hopper had been intently watching the fuel pressure and quantity gages when he suddenly yelled to the pilot in an accelerated southern drawl, "That old number two tank is givin' out ...pressure is below fifty and droppin' fast."

"What's it been, about forty five minutes?"

Hopper nodded vigorously.

Hank Weston turned to half-face Haysus and said, "Stand by the fuel transfer switches; use both sets of Tokyo tanks." Then to the co-pilot, "Hop, say when you want to make the transfer."

Jordan stared at the gages in front of him. After a long two minutes, turned to Haysus and shouted, "Ready Haysus? NOW."

As soon as the switches were manipulated, number three engine off to the right, coughed once, then re-fired and continued to join the chorus of four huge power plants churning into the stygian night. Another ten minutes passed with ice noisily skipping off the outer skin of the B-17 amid the buffeting caused by the unstable air of the storm when suddenly the airplane broke clear of the disturbance. Bracken Davids in the plexiglass nose yelled into the intercom, "You guys! Do you see what I see? By God, Stars. We're out of it. Nice going Hank."

The altimeter showed their altitude was slightly higher than 14,000 feet, so Hank eased the control column forward, walked back the throttles to an airspeed reading of 140 and heaved a deep breath. On the intercom, "Pilot to engineer. Haysus, the fuel should be gone from the number two tank. Have a look from your top turret with a flashlight."

The flight engineer disconnected his oxygen and squirmed into the upper turret where he again utilized the oxygen system and intercom at that position.

"Engineer to pilot, over."

"Go ahead Haysus, has the gas stopped spraying?"

"That's a roger. That old tank must be as dry as a gourd."

Luke hearing the exchange from the flight deck up front, knew that Weston and Hopper would continue to be concerned with nursing the remaining fuel in the system. Each massive one thousand horsepower Wright engine consumed gasoline at about 54 gallons an hour. At normal cruising speed!

Both pilots did focus their attention on the fuel gages as the B-17 droned east toward what appeared to be a diminishing of darkness on the horizon. Though maintaining an altitude of 14,000 feet it was possible in this sixth hour into the flight to be aware of the thinning of the cloud cover below them. At this point, O'Mally in the ball confirmed the fuel no longer leaked.

"Radio, this is Navigator. Luke, get me a fix from Meek's Field or Valley radio range, Over."

"Radio here, Wilco."

Luke managed to contact a station with the fixed antennae on the first effort. After receiving the QDM he relayed the position and course to George L. In an obviously confident voice the navigator asked the pilot to alter the course just four degrees to the north.

Within thirty minutes the pilots on the flight deck were aware of an orange orb peeking at them on the edge of the horizon almost dead ahead. And below, the clouds only thinly veiled the earth where most eyes in the B-17 could catch a glimpse of the ocean...or was it the Irish Sea? Hank asked himself.

Then over the intercom, "Pilot to crew." We have contacted Valley Control at Valley Wales on the command set. We're clear to make our approach if we can find any dry land. We'll be lucky if Billy can fill his cigarette lighter with the fuel in these tanks right now. So sit tight."

There was no response from the crew as the gunners were all straining to catch sight of land; any solid ground would do. Now it was time for Luke to ask the Meek's station for a

QFE, the barometric pressure reading from Valley, a necessity in order to re- set the altimeter for landing. As soon as this information was relayed to the flight deck, Hank banked sharply entering a scattering of clouds while passing through 10,000 feet.

"Pilot to crew, it's okay to go off oxygen." Every man unsnapped his mask, the clammy rubber device having accumulated some condensed moisture on the inside. Now the altimeter read 9,000 feet, then 8,000, finally crossing over the green coast of northwest Britain, the pilot once more contacted the control tower at the airfield at Valley, Wales. He quickly leveled off at 3,000 feet, well beneath the random fluffy clouds. Hank Weston then spoke with authority, "All crew members to the radio room and brace yourselves, NOW." Everyone except for Haysus whose presence was always required on the flight deck, complied.

Hank then spoke to the tower. "Valley, this is silver dollar three niner six two. Request permission to land straightaway. We have QFE, over.

Back came a well modulated, distinctly British female voice. "Three niner six two, we're expecting you. You are cleared to land on runway 035. Welcome to the UK. Over."

"Thanks very much. Out."

Quickly, immediately after the roar of the two remaining working engines were switched off, on that signal, the aircraft was filled with excited chatter. Finally completely relieved, the gunners tried to top each other as the tension was relaxed, since land was visible and an apparent safe landing eminent. Meanwhile, the B-17 reached final approach.Abruptly, the number two engine coughed once, sputtered and died. Hopper immediately hit the feathering button causing the propeller blades to turn at right angles with the engine to prevent undue drag.

Hank Weston gripped he control yoke until his knuckles turned white, both feet tense on the rudder petals as he completed his turn on the final here was the runway, straight ahead. Good! As the macadam surface rose to meet the huge aircraft, the number one engine expired so now both engines on the left were gone. Losing all power on the port side caused enormous torque pulling the aircraft off center of gravity. Both pilots held a true course by literally wrestling the machine, as Hank worked back the throttles with his right hand so that the B-17 hit the tarmac with a screeching of tires coinciding with an uncharacteristic bump and a bounce. The flight was ended for crew and airplane after brakes were applied as per regulation, and they were able to exit the main runway successfully and remarkably, managed to taxi with the two remaining live engines to an assigned hard stand. The pilots looked at each other's sweat-drenched coveralls, laughed nervously and shook hands. Immediately, Weston grabbed the always important Form One sheet on which he entered the information written large regarding the faulty gas tank cap in this B- 17 That information will be the first thing observed by the ground mechanics at this particular Air Field.

From the gunners as the two working engines were turned off, came a chorus of excited "yahoos, yeah man" and enthusiastic pounding of each other's backs. Finally, as they all disembarked with their personal authorized equipment, every man now suddenly somber, knew that their really serious trials would begin soon, when they entered combat.

Before leaving the airplane, Luke Lewis entered in his radio operator's log which would be submitted to American Base operations at Valley :

Date: September 30, 1944. Landed Valley Wales under reduced power, 1049 GMT

He then signed off, by adding his signature.

* * * *

FATAL MISCHIEF
Silencing the Mouth of Trumpet Lily

*Fox Hunter tooting hunting horn to recall the hounds
after the chase is over. (a normal ritual.)*

Prologue By Author

This short story is a fictional depiction of real people. Most of the names of people herein are quasi - inventions, lives which I have assigned. So, there may be some resemblance to real people, most of whom, sadly, are long gone. With two exceptions, town and city names are fictional. The major setting for this story, Portageville, is made up, though it resembles a real village in northwest Missouri. The fox hunting magazine, *The Red Ranger*, actually existed and was prominent among large numbers of subscribing fox hunters and conservationists during the first half of the twentieth century.

Most importantly, the hunters unique thrill of the sport of fox hunting was enjoyed widely by "forks of the creek" foxhunters in America during those years, (as distinguished from those aristocratic fox hunters who rode horseback following the hounds.) Clearly evident was the passion for these remarkable American Foxhounds by famous breeders and hunters alike. Every fox hunter's affection and outright love and protection of their animals including the much maligned fox, is a part of the lore of that most unique outdoor sporting event in American history.

* * * *

That morning as I was about to leave our house for school,

I beheld there on the front porch one of Dad 's prize fox hounds lying on her side, stiffened legs pumping. I recall also hearing the agonizing whimpering sounding from a mouth dripping foamy saliva. Glassy eyes rolled up to me while I stood, my heart pounding, there in the doorway. She was pleading for the help that I, a fifth-grader, knew was beyond anything I could do.

Trumpet Lily, a beautiful black and white pure bred hound of the reliable Trumbo strain, died there on the porch seconds after Dad appeared to take in the horrible scene. His face, dark, turning white with the emotions of anger and compassion, gritted through his teeth a single word: "Poisoned !" I couldn't know at the time, nor could by father, that serious consequences would follow in our community of only some six hundred residents in the ensuing immediate years to come.

* * * *

In the year nineteen thirty, when I had reached the age of seven my father, Francis Lewis, had allowed me to accompany him on a few night-time fox hunts. Today, in the first decade of the twenty first century, that sport has been reduced in numbers to a mere sprinkling of serious hunters in the United States. Several factors including, mainly, burgeoning population in formerly rural areas created the diminishing number of red foxes, foxhounds and people who once loved that most endearing humane activity.

Chasing the elusive fox has been a sport in England for hundreds of years. Well-to-do land owners in The North American Colonies were also avid hunters of the red and more rare gray foxes. The English foxhound was imported in significant numbers during the seventeenth and eighteenth centuries. Our pre-eminent founding father, George Washington, owned packs of foxhounds and enjoyed immensely the chase on horseback across the countryside of Virginia. It is recorded that he specifically reveled in the "music" of the hounds sounding their distinct "mouth" after a fox was struck. In those days, and even now in certain parts of England and the United States, following the chase aboard a fine piece of horse flesh was and is an important part of the hunt.

The English breeds were rather stocky specimens of the foxhound, in contrast to the American bred animals. When viewed side by side, it would be evident to most casual observers that the American breeds had longer legs, were slimmer, with well developed hips and thighs. Most breeds were also endowed with apparently capacious chest cavities. Delicate ears, not too short or excessively long fall beautifully on either side of an intelligent head. At maturity they will stand at least two feet at the shoulder. Most pure breeds had tails that were neither flag- like nor smooth rat tailed. Something in between might best describe that expressive ornament. Running at full tilt nose close to the ground, every dog in the chase carries its tail curving up over the back. However, all these physical features are secondary to the sensitive nose, drive and the cry when in the race. Bonus features include its loving nature with the master and the beautiful eyes that range from brown to gold and occasionally to blue. The American foxhound when all is said and done. is bred to chase foxes and to cry distinctively making its statement to the listening world during the race. Frankly, the Trumbo, Walker or July strains were built for speed and endurance in contrast to its progenitors of England. Of course the breeders were also always working on improving the mouth or cry of the hound, a task that was almost impossible to achieve. Adult hounds, therefore, would sound the high notes emitted in full cry by a "bitch" (though that term by owners was rarely used, preferring instead to address a female animal as "little miss or lady".) Pure bred printed pedigrees listed the female along the linage as the dam. One would see the various generations in a given pedigree defining the sex as sire and dam. Adult male foxhounds would normally have a distinctive baritone chopping sound, some bordering on a gruff tone.

However, pedigree registrations never asked to identify the important "cry" feature in an animal as such descriptions would vary from one owner's ear to the next. Fox hunters in my time were pleased when a yearling pup graduated from chasing rabbits in the area and began to join the pack in a race and would let everyone know that youngster was in the chase. Moreover, if and when that hound sounded off, whether emitting a sound like a chop, a squeal, tenor bay or a lower pitched chopping baritone ...every animal could be identified. Usually they could be placed by the listening hunters in an approximate position in the pack. The best analogy hunters have used to describe the sport is like "watching" a horse race with your ears only. Usually a fox chase might be sighted during the early daylight hours, only at organized group fox hunts.

My father was editor and publisher of the leading fox hunting magazine in America during the first three decades of the twentieth century. He and most of his subscribers chose to transport their hounds to a favorite wooded area where there was known to be a habitat for foxes. Very few readers of the *Red Ranger Magazine* would ride horses to the hounds. The term those sportsmen used to delineate this practice was a term my father invented, "forks of the creek" hunters. Thus, the hunters would drive to a relatively remote area, usually around sun down, preferably after a rain shower with little or no wind blowing, when the scent of the fox will rise gently off its trail. There the hunters would open the door of the portable crates and "cast" the hounds. It was rarely necessary for any of the hunters to "whip" a dog to direct it in a specific direction. You see, there was always a leader, an educated striker or two in the pack of foxhounds who would know instinctively what direction to advance, alert, nose to the ground, tail curled above its hind quarters. If the fox scent is fresh the hound will sound off, a cry that would, in effect say, "here it is…follow me!" Soon the entire pack would join in the chase.

Customarily after the hounds have scattered and before the fox is "struck" the hunters would gather the twigs and kindling to start a small camp fire. A half-gallon bucket of coffee would be suspended over or near the crackling fire and a little later the snack of sandwiches made by wives would be munched by most of the hunters. Meanwhile quiet conversation would fill the lull…topics usually concerning the comradeship all shared in this sport,. until the first mouthing cry from the darkness is sounded.

Always, eventually one of the hunters having strolled beyond the light coming from the campfire, would whisper loudly, "Listen." The other hunters would rise from where they were seated on logs and look in the direction the first hunter was pointing indicating the area from which the cry of the strike dog was sounded. If the hound were not on a cold trail, later there were other voices to be heard as the pack began to gather and the chase would begin. The crescendo eventually sounds nearer, then as the experienced red fox, obviously enjoying the game, would often tend to lead the hounds in a wide circle, sometimes going out of hearing. Eventually, after almost two hours, the fox would seek its den at which point the hunt for that night would be ended. Never, in my experience growing up with these forks of the creek fox hunters throughout the states of Missouri and Kansas, did I witness the destruction of a red fox. It was apparent to me during all those years of my youth taking part in these hunts, that the hounds seemed to be aware that the game was in the chase. When the fox did go "to ground," most of the hounds would come straggling back to where they were released, tongues out dripping, against a lower jaw. Now and then, my father might choose to take up his horn and blow a few toots to encourage his hounds to come back. The horn many hunters used was an adaptation from a steer's horn that had been expertly carved at the small end to form a convenient mouth piece. Remarkably, hounds would respond to the tooting of the hunter's horn by their master.

A striking difference from the elite horseback hunters in this country and in England is that the hunters horn used abroad would often be a brass instrument. Also, it seems that the horn during those hunts would be used to encourage the more reluctant hounds to proceed apace, so to speak, not to call them back.

Our village, Portageville, located in a valley along the bluffs of the Missouri River in northwest Missouri, was bounded by timber on most of two sides. The hills and hollows provided an ideal environment for the Red Fox. It was convenient I thought, that my parents had selected a house just on the town side of the slope that descended from the dense part of the wooded area.

The reason I refer to our living in the vicinity of fox country is that for Dad and for his close hunter friends, all we had to do was release the usually eight to ten hounds from their kennel beyond the back yard, the chosen night for the hunt. All the animals knew how to wheel right and scoot up the hill into the woods. Thus, from an early age I was often permitted to be included. It was always a thrill when my father said, "Tim, put on your warm clothes, we're hunting." After more than sixty years I can still smell the compelling, smokey- pungent, almost musk-like fragrance of Dad's hunting clothes. My first hunt there in the nearby woods found me trembling with excitement walking up he narrow path so that my dad had to lift me, just barely seven years old, onto his back while he carried the kerosine lantern which cast strange appearing shadows. However, mysteriously, there were a few nights when the hunters were heading out on foot chugging up into the timber, I was told I should stay home. When I had become an adult, around the time of World War II, I learned why my father at certain times instructed me to stay home with mother. The reason? It seems that I might be left at home when an occasional hunter, who was prone to abuse profanity, joined the hunt. My dad naively just wished to shelter his youngest son from hearing certain profane expletives.

When World War II ended, Dad took me and one of my close friends hunting one evening. Also in the group was a veteran of the First World War and a part- time hunter. By then, my friend and I having been in the military and had traveled half way around the world and back had picked up language that one in those days did not use in most polite societies. We younger men that night were encouraged to open up regarding some of our war experiences. So as my friend began to colorfully describe an event, I secretly remembered my father's feeling about certain "cuss words." Of course the vet from the WW I also had some "off color" expressions. Having always been circumspect with my language around my parents, I must confess to being a bit embarrassed. Sort of like hearing cussing in church? So I was glad when the hounds finally did strike the trail of a fox and conversation in those veins ceased.

At the close of every successful hunt, when the last of the tired dogs returned to camp, wet from cooling off in puddles or a running spring, it was time to go. Hunters made sure the camp fire was extinguished, then we would retrace our steps through the woods down the path toward home and kennel with the hounds usually leading the way.

If, the fox hunt took place several miles away from home, there was always the chance that one or two eager hounds might not return in a timely manner to the casting area. When this happened after an indeterminate waiting period, the hunters would load up the returnees for the ride back to Portageville. I can recall many cases when a missing hound would find its way home by the next day, extremely tired and hungry, but safe. As with other hunting breeds, the American Foxhound possessed a remarkable gyro compass in its system which it used to reach home base. Most of us of a certain age will remember the story of *Balto*, and the famous heroic tale of how that lead Husky led the sled dog team all the way to Nome in an Alaskan blizzard when his owner-musher lost his way...thus remarkably delivering the vital life saving serum. I am persuaded that the foxhound also has that same wonderful faculty.

* * * *

After the local Deputy Sheriff, Jim McKinney, examined the lifeless *Trumpet Lily*, listened to my father relate the circumstances, and took a statement the animal was buried back beyond the garage. Of course, by then I was in class at school. The following is a narration of dramatic events that took place in those days covering a period of a little more than two years in our town.

For weeks afterward, the collection of fox hunters debated the incident but without any resolution. Though the town deputy had very little on his calendar, he spent no time investigating the case. After all, he thought, we are talking about an animal, for God's sake. But in the minds of the hunters there was much speculation and an occasional pointing of fingers, naming names of possible offenders. however, accusations were contained and for a time discreet.

It was assumed that in the case of *Trumpet Lily*, it was bad luck for her to have been one of those fox hounds that did not return after a chase the night before. In the process of finding her way back home she had apparently found a bone or piece of meat that had been laced with one of the available poisons of the day, strychnine or arsenic At least that was the conclusion the fox hunting community unanimously endorsed.

Not having the skills of discovery or hardly more than suspicions, some of the hunters began to name possible sources of the heartless deed. One person, a Sam Tarott, came to mind. Tarott was a rather reclusive sort who lived on the edge of town and was seen, (it was said) kicking someone's dog when the animal chanced to cross by his doorstep. He and his woman were relatively new to the community and he made their living as a day laborer, obviously this was scant evidence and was a bit hard to make the giant leap to the administering of poison to a passing hound.

Another person whose name surfaced among the hound owners as perpetrator was a woman who lived in a very old, impressively large house located a half mile north and east of the small business district on main street. Myrtle Manning lived alone and maintained the property with the occasional aid of youngsters who would try to contain the growth of grass, weeds and a forest of shrubs. It was assumed that Myrtle had once been married but few people knew anything about her personal life. No one in town was ever invited to the home. Her shopping for groceries and other necessities was accomplished on foot and took place, apparently only once a week. She rarely spoke to people except when she did her parsimonious shopping. Again, her "strange" behavior was the only reason she was suspected.

Lastly, another suspect was one of the local blacksmiths, a large man named Sagerson. His shop was down town but at the east end of the shopping area. The house in which he lived was near the top of one of the highest hills in town but easily within walking distance of his shop. A wife took care of his house and prepared his meals but it was Lamis Sagerson who invariably did the shopping in town. Few people knew anything at all about the wife. Of course she was seen about town from time to time but rarely went out of her way to speak or socialize with other women. A main reason for some of the hunters to point to Sagerson was that when an animal of any kind came near his shop he would literally chase it out,often throwing odd pieces of metal at the poor beast. It didn't matter if it were a curious cat, dog or a wandering racoon.

Months later, the following spring, a local hunter named Alex Tarpin found one of his foxhounds stricken in a similar manner. It seems that his dog was found dead in a ditch between his property and a tiny stream known as Frakes Run. Now Mckinney, the deputy, exhibited a modicum of interest, though it had been months since the Lewis dog had been poisoned. This time he did make some notes, using a stub of a pencil and a small spiral note pad.

When Deputy Mckinney asked Tarpin if he could recall any reason why the dog was killed, Tarpin had no idea. Scratching his balding head, he responded that he had released the animal for some exercise along the creek and the animal must have "wandered or chased the scent of a fox somewheres The poor dog, in Tarpin's mind, found a piece of meat and consumed it. Certainly it was indeed obvious from the evidence, that his hound had been poisoned as had the Francis Lewis hound. Deputy Mckinney looked once more on the stiffened remains folded the notebook and put away the pencil and said, "Let me know if you have any more problems."

By then, a few of the neighbors had gathered and stood around shaking their heads in concern for Tarpin's loss. As the deputy departed Alex Tarpin fiercely spat on the ground and muttered his obvious disappointment "Someone in this here town has got a problem. and I don't know why"

Tarpin was not a close confidant of Francis Lewis. But he did bring his three hounds along when some of the others headed out on a hunt. And of course he read every monthly issue of *the Red Ranger.* He worked as a section hand on the nearby Burlington Railroad and was normally a congenial person who was well liked in the community. The same could be said of Lewis who also had almost universal respect. Maintaining his magazine publishing business out of the office on main street was an important economic advantage for the small town and its post office. Did someone have a score to settle against the owners of the hounds or was someone in Portageville simply exercising a deep and abiding hatred for hounds? No one at that time had an answer...

Of course, Lewis had little time to take from his business during an ordinary day to visit with his hunter friends. Filling the posts of editor and publisher was too time consuming to allow him to deviate even momentarily from his daily tasks. It was only evenings at the campfire on a hunt when he was able to absorb the speculation surrounding the poisoning of Trumpet Lily and the one owned by Alex Tarpin.

* * * *

With the advent of autumn in the nineteen - thirtees and forties, Nellie and Francis Lewis would load their family in the car and drive the two hundred miles or so south to a town in the Missouri Ozarks. This annual event was sponsored and arranged by the Missouri State Foxhunters Association. Francis Lewis was the founding Secretary and the officer who did the planning. During that week he would arrange for an employee to feed and water his hounds in the kennel as he did not think it appropriate for him to take his dogs to the meet where there would be competitive races and bench shows. For the Lewis kids it was a real vacation and for all the hunters it was a week long frenzy of visiting, laughter, early morning fox chases, sleepless nights and plenty of stories. Often, fox hunters from Texas would bring their mounts to the meet location, this particular year at Mountain Grove, Missouri… so that they could act as judges while actually following the running hounds while riding horseback. All the foxhounds competing would be marked with a number painted on each flank. Of course trophies or ribbons were awarded to the owners of the best hounds. Towns, usually in the Missouri Ozarks, vied in those years to host these events. Of course, the fox hunters were always well behaved and usually free spenders. At the end of the week's events, the member hunters reluctantly headed back to their respective homes.

When the Lewis family arrived home in Portageville late in the day, the phone by the radio stand was ringing the minute Nellie Lewis and we youngsters entered the back door. She lifted the receiver and heard a man's voice ask if Mister Lewis was home. Calling her husband who was unloading some of the tent gear and bags, she handed the instrument to him as he entered that room. After a congenial greeting into the mouthpiece of the telephone, his face became grim, "Did you get in touch with McKinney?" A pause. Then he spoke again. "Give me some time, we just got home. Right, Come to my office in one hour." Within less than an hour, Francis Lewis had completed the task of unloading the car, glanced out to the kennel where his hounds, tails wagging showing their pleasure at his return. It took him only five minutes more to walk the short distance to the main street where he unlocked the door to his office.

Very shortly, he was joined by the man who phoned him, an obviously agitated, florid faced Alex Tarpin. Lewis waved him over to an inner office where he pulled the on-off cord to the light hanging from the ceiling. When they were both seated, Lewis leaned forward and said, "What's this Alex, about another one of your hounds?"

Tarpin rubbed his palms on his overall clad thighs. "It's my *Rajah* dog, Mister Lewis, three days ago I found him in my back yard, dead. Poisoned. In three months I've lost two thirds of my pack, and I'm plenty mad." At this unseemly outburst, Alex bowed his head and looked away. "You asked me on the phone if McKinney knows. Yeah, he knows. I went straight to his house and told him but he don't know nothing…, 'cept he can manage to pick up a drunk on Main Street and take him to jail at the county seat. Seems he just can't get too concerned about our hounds."

Lewis didn't interrupt until Tarpin finished with this question…"I just don't know where to turn. Can we get the law to at least make an effort to investigate these crimes?"

"Alex, I am just as upset and angry about all this as you. They got my *Trumpet Lily* first, as you know. Tomorrow I'll talk to Mckinney an let you know what I learn, I promise." With that the editor rose from his chair and led the way out the front door. The two men shook hands. Tarpin with downcast head, donned his cap and ambled, head down, up the street toward his home down by the creek. Lewis, paused for just another instant to return to his desk where he gave a cursory look at the accumulated mail placed there by his secretary. As the hour was near meal time, he turned out the light, locked up and walked home.

Nellie Lewis was as devoted to the hounds and hunting as her husband, though it was mostly vicarious. For the most part, most of what she knew of the sport was from the pages of her husband's magazine, *The Red Ranger*. However, she truly loved her husband and felt a certain kinship with the local fox hunters and all those she knew on a regional basis in Missouri. When Francis reported his conversation on the phone and later that evening in the office, she felt a deep and abiding sorrow for the man, Tarpin. He was a widower so there was no social connection on her part with his family since he was also childless. At the supper table that night over coffee after the children had excused themselves, she finally asked, "Do you think it will ever end?"

"The deliberate killing of hounds? I can tell you this, Nellie dear, some of the hunters around here are at the flash point. If the law doesn't show some kind of effort toward solving this rash of insane acts, something's going to blow up." With that the grim faced man banged the saucer on which he placed his now empty coffee cup.

From his office the next morning, Lewis phoned Deputy Sheriff McKinney, asking him if he would mind stopping by the *Red Ranger* office that day. The deputy readily agreed to be there a little before noon. True to his word, McKinney entered the office only minutes after the girls in the office had left for their noon hour break.

The two men sat facing each other across the desk in the back office. Lewis got right to the point: "Jim, as you may know, I've been away all week and just got home last night. The minute I arrived I learned that Tarpin lost another foxhound. That makes three local hounds poisoned that I know of...one of mine and two others owned by Alex. I guess we are wondering if you have any leads as to who the perpetrator might be." The deputy sat upright looking over the editor's shoulder at a print on the opposite wall depicting *Custer's Last Stand*. Lewis continued. "For a small town we have some dedicated, proud hunters and owners of fairly expensive foxhounds here and a number outside of town in your jurisdiction whom I hope to contact today or tomorrow."

McKinney's eyes finally found the editor's and slowly shook his head. This was all new to him so it was obvious that he really did not know how to proceed in the matter of, what would you call it, multiple *canineicide?* He finally opened his mouth, scratched his ear and said, "Mister Lewis, I will be honest with you, I don't have the slightest inkling where to start looking. Do I depend on hearsay, rumor or what ?"

Francis Lewis looked long at the bland features of the slope shouldered uniformed man seated across from him. A polished badge was pinned on the left breast pocket of his brown shirt and a holstered hand gun was suspended from a wide belt. He held his hat in one hand by its wide brim. "I know one thing for sure Deputy J im, we expect you to look at the total picture here in Portageville. There can't be many folks around here who would deliberately go out and poison an animal…any animal, let alone an innocent, probably valuable foxhound. These are not "cur dogs" with doubtful ancestry that's being killed, for the most part they come from a long line of well bred animals. Also, hunters often count them as part of the family because of the sheer joy they impart when they are doing what they have been bred to do… chase the fox and give a wondrous cry while doing it. I will also suggest that the sheriff, your boss, up at the county seat would back you up in the investigation." Lewis reached for a pencil, rolled it between his hands then leaned back in his swivel chair Actually he knew McKinney could not relate to the thrill of the hunt he just briefly described. So he was hoping that by invoking the authority of Sheriff Tom Cummings whom Lewis had supported in the past three elections, it might help to motivate Mckinney.

The deputy straightened up, shifted the hat to his other hand and now looked directly at the editor. "Give me a few more days Mister Lewis. I think I know as much about the incidents as you and Tarpin know at this time. I'll get back to you after you have got in touch with the other fox hunters you mentioned, Okay?"

"Absolutely, Jim. If we all keep our eyes open and our ears alert, someone may give you some solid information. Thanks very much for coming in today. I'll report back to Alex later today when he gets off work." The Deputy Sheriff rose and shook the proffered hand Lewis extended. Carefully positioning his hat he exited the editor's private office and went out the front door.

After dinner at the Lewis house that noon, Francis turned to the phone and contacted the other foxhound owners and hunters in the county. All were farmers of small acreages. He asked each if their hounds were all healthy. In every case, each person was confident that all were safe and accounted for. They all were acutely aware of the three stricken hounds in the town of Portageville and sympathetic with Lewis and Tarpin. Next he either talked to or left messages at the homes of the other three hunters who lived in Portageville. He managed to reach Colin Bracken, Pleas Largent and HarryFielding. Old Cranford, the local part time hunter, also wanted to be at the meeting. Finally, Lewis made a note to phone Alex Tarpin that evening.

For most of the autumn season that year, the area was experiencing a dry spell so there was an extended respite from chasing the red fox for the hounds and hunters,.who required moisture for the scent of the fox to rise from the trail. Consequently the next evening all the hunters that Lewis had phoned, were free to assemble in his office on Main Street in Portageville. Nellie Lewis had provided two percolators of coffee and a batch of her oatmeal cookies for the informal meeting. After the small talk had simmered down, and waiting until all the men had found a chair and a place to put their coffee cups, Francis Lewis opened the meeting by standing by his desk, to his height of a full six feet… saying, "You all know what's been going on here. My *Trumpet Lily* was the first to be fed some poison. As tragic as it was to me, a person would think that her horrible death would be just an isolated instance. But you all know now that Alex," he swept his arm toward the stern -faced man in overalls and denim jacket sitting next to Colin Bracken, well, he "lost *Rajah*, and another hound, right Alex?"

Tarpin glanced at Lewis and responded, "Yeah, my little *Lady Bug*." Lewis then, seated himself, swung his chair, looked around the room, took off his glasses and rubbed his eyes. His lanky frame, still in his white shirt with the celluloid collar and tie, contrasted with the casual work clothes worn by the assembled fox hunter friends. Finally he reported his conversation with Deputy Mckinny and asked for reactions and/or opinions from everyone. Gradually, the men began to open up.

One by one, the hunters expressed deep and rancorous outrage at the offenses. The three farmer hunters were more restrained but completely supportive in whatever measures were required to apprehend the perpetrator or perpetrators, for as Pleas Largent suggested, "There might be more than one guilty person hereabouts." That thought reawakened the names of the three local people who for months, some had believed guilty of the heartless acts. Plain language with an occasional descriptive expletive directed toward whomever might be guilty was expressed during the meeting. Finally it was apparent to all that everyone should be watchful. Lewis ended the extraordinary meeting with the advice that they should cooperate with Deputy McKinny in his "investigation." Honestly, there were no other reasonable options proposed at this time, as the meeting ended on that apocryphal note.

As Deputy Jim McKinny promised he would do, after Lewis gathered the fox hunters for that private assembly in the *Red Ranger* office, he came to see the editor two days following the meeting of the fox hunters. Lewis led him to the private office in back where he took the offered seat by the side of the desk. "Mr. Lewis. this is one strange case. I have been looking around and quietly asked some questions here and there. Someone suggested that I ought to interrogate a couple of people but I've been told you have to have some evidence of a motive to go that route." The editor's response was only with an agreeable nod of his head. Then he spoke.

"Jim, I just want to tell you that the fox hunters, to a man, are getting mighty edgy. Now don't take that the wrong way…they just want to get to the bottom of this mystery. As you know, I am certainly not a lawyer or an investigator, but it seems to me that you might first go to the hardware store to ask who, if anyone, has acquired any kind of poison within the past six months or so. Farmers and even townspeople pick up strychnine or even arsenic for the control of rats and more often arsenate of lead for tobacco worms. You know? Either one of those products would be fatal if consumed by a hound, even when administered in minute quantities."

McKinny narrowed his eyes, looked over to the editor and said, "I can't believe I haven't thought of that. I'll get right on it." With that astonishing admission, the deputy jammed his hat on his head, patted his holstered gun and left the office.

The dry season extended that year into winter which brought moisture early in December in the form of snow. Totally uncharacteristically for Missouri, the snow persisted well into January. So the foxhunting season did not open up again until late February. Hounds and hunters were itching to go. Having languished in kennels all winter, the hounds needed some action. On the appointed evening, a small group of men brought their hounds to the large Lewis back yard. When the Lewis hounds were turned out of the kennel, all the others were released so that more than fifteen animals, including Alex Tarpin's sole surviving hound, burst forth, all bounding upland into the timber above Portageville. It was quite cool, though the snow had melted, soaking the fallen leaves and grasses. The men had barely managed to find enough dry bark and limbs to make a camp fire, when the first opening cry was sounded. It continued long enough so that many of the other hounds soon joined the choir. There were warblers, squealers, chop mouths, yodelers and every mouth in between thus identifying the individual hounds giving chase. After the red fox chose to seek his den, more than two hours had elapsed. Very soon the dogs began to return to the hunters. Most of them.

It was a very successful hunt, the men concluded. Comments about the performance of certain hounds and the chase dominated the conversation as everyone descended the hill to town.

The following morning, Francis Lewis was in the front office reviewing the print schedule for the magazine. Deputy McKinney came through the door and in a low voice, said to the editor. "I think I have some reliable information about the dog poisoning, Mr. Lewis. Can we talk?"

Lewis looked into the grim face of the deputy, nodded and led the way to the private office in back. "What do you have, Jim?" Neither man seated himself as McKinney paced around the desk.

"I followed your advice and had an interesting conversation with old man Mott at the hardware store. I didn't let on that I was doing an investigation, but in just hangin' around I asked him about business. Then I saw a cabinet door with, you know, a kind of red letter X on the outside. I knew in a minute that right there is where Mott stored any poison. Sure enough while I was standin' there lookin' he mentioned that he has to keep arsenate of lead and other such stuff up away from people casually coming in contact with it."

Lewis, waiting patiently for the deputy to make his point, stood with his arms folded. He said, "So, go on Jim."

"I asked Mr. Mott, who in the world around here buys that stuff anyway; you know, just makin' conversation. He mentioned the names of a couple of farmers, over toward the river, and then you know who he named?" Now he leaned close and just above a whisper, "one of his Portageville customers, the blacksmith feller!"

Lewis, at that point, took a chair and motioned Deputy McKinney to be seated also. "Jim, do you think this is sufficient evidence to call Lamis Sagerson to task for killing our dogs? Seems to me in order for the prosecuting attorney to direct you to arrest and have the state try the man we need something more. Am I right on this?"

"I reckon so. Anyway, I plan to get up to the county seat and talk to Sheriff Cummings about all this to see what he suggests." With that, the two men left the private office, bid each other goodby as the deputy said over his shoulder leaving the building, "I'll see you later."

Before he had an opportunity to pass McKinney's information to the local fox hunters, Alex Tarpin burst into the office, red face contorted with rage, and headed for the private office in the rear of the *Red Ranger* building. Lewis hurried after him, opening the door and motioned the obviously agitated man inside. "Alex, what's going on?" Tarpin slammed his cap on the desk in front of him and growled, now they got my last hound. Poisoned, like the others. Why, Mister Lew, why?" He sobbed the question.

Francis Lewis had to take a seat. "Your last hound, Alex? This is just terrible. Are you saying that *Dandy* didn't make it back to us after the hunt the other night." Alex nodded his head, the corners of his mouth curved down and wiping his eyes.

"In a voice that sounded strained he replied, "He made it back to my front door and there is where I found him just a little while ago. Dead. Like the all the others. I just couldn't go to work my shift today."

"Alex," Lewis spoke softly, "this is small consolation, but McKinney thinks he has a lead on the person responsible for all these killings. I just found out. He told me he was going to check with Cummings at the court house before he proceeds any furtherSo maybe we can solve these cases, eventually."

Tarpin raised his head, looking directly at the editor, "What kind of lead? Does he have someone in mind?" These questions asked in a voice that shook, but softly. At that point Francis Lewis regretted mentioning that there could be a suspect perpetrator. But he felt he was honor bound to mention Sagerson as a suspect. Alex Tarpin deserved to be aware of all the known facts.

So Lewis outlined the information McKinney reported earlier, emphasizing that the evidence right now is circumstantial. "We'll know more when the deputy returns from the Court House."

Alex Tarpin lifted his head, looked steadily into the editor's eyes, rubbed the moisture from his eyes with his big fists and uttered one word. "Sagerson!" Lewis then repeated the information that Deputy McKinney will bring a course of action, if any, when he returns to Portageville later that day. Tarpin heaved himself out of the chair, mumbled "Thanks Mister Lew," and without offering his hand, left the building.

Francis Lewis felt a deep hurt and compassion for Alex

Tarpin. Looking back, since the loss of his first hound, it seemed as if the formerly robust, vigorous man who was somewhere around fifty five years old had visibly aged. Of course, over the past year and a half he had seen more of Alex than in the preceding decade. Lewis thought, my old *Sissy Bell* will be producing a litter of pups, sired by *Champion Honest Fred*...I'll make him a gift of his pick of the litter. When will they be whelped? Eight weeks or so. Concluding those thoughts he went back to his desk and finally gave some attention to putting together next month's issue of *The Red Ranger*.

That evening after supper, Francis related to Nellie the conversations in his office that day. He also told of his thoughts of providing Alex Tarpin with one of their forthcoming litter of pups. She smiled in agreement. "I'm so sorry for him. Those hounds were the only living things he had to his name."

The next morning, Francis Lewis was up early, had walked to his office building and was about to unlock the entrance door. His pocket watch indicated that the time was a little before eight, when he heard a voice calling from up near the bank building. "Hey Lew, Lew... Francis! There's been a shootin." It was Pleas Largent who had called and was hurrying up the sidewalk toward the editor's office. Both men entered the building. Inside, just beyond the door, both men stood face to face, Largent was breathing hard and his countenance was pale as he shook his head from side to side.

Lewis took his arm and led him to a table off to one side where they found two chairs. Seated, Pleas put his elbows on the table, looked at the editor and said, "Lew, it is just terrible. Someone shot the blacksmith. I just came from Sagersen's shop ...I had some welding he was doing for me...and there he was bent over a saw horse. Didn't even have his work apron on. I could tell he was dead. He must have been killed the minute he reached his shop this morning."

"Did you, or has anyone, called a doctor, or Deputy McKinney? He must have finished his business at the Court House yesterday and is in town by now."

Pleas shook his head. "You're the first person on the street that I've seen. If you can reach Doc Carter, I'll look up McKinney." Lewis nodded and went to the phone as Largent hurriedly left the office.

No more than twenty minutes had elapsed before Lewis was joined by Largent, the Doctor and finally driving up, Deputy Jim McKinney. The four men descended on the blacksmith shop where, just as Pleas had reported, the massive body of Lamis Sagerson was indeed sprawled across a wooden saw horse near his cold forge. First the doctor examined the body, under the scrutiny of the deputy. "One clean wound," Doctor Carter said, "and obviously fatal. Right between the eyes!"

This homicide turned out to be the first such crime in that town ever committed in the memory of the oldest citizens of Portageville. Obviously it was on the minds of all who knew about it. And that included everyone in that part of town, well before the removal of the body by a funeral director in Hill City, Kansas across the Missouri River five miles away. By mid-day a good-sized contingent of officers and investigators had arrived on the scene. Looking for clues and questioning anyone within shouting distance of the black smith shop. It was beginning to sprinkle a fine trace of rain.

Sheriff Tom Cummings, having driven down from the county seat, and his deputy, McKinney, were obviously in charge attempting to isolate those in town who may have had a problem with Sagerson. Truthfully, Sagerson had few friends in town since his disposition was usually surly or at the best, unpleasant. So not that many locals were grieving over the demise of the smithy, with the obvious exception of his wife who was when informed of the shooting, quite overcome with shock. About two hours into the milling about of the lawmen and others, a lone figure slowly plodded up the gravel road that connected the main street in town to the bridge over the creek. That road also led to the houses down by the creek. Standing on the periphery of the group surrounding the sheriff, the late arrival, Alex Tarpin, his denim shirt damp from the rain, called out, "It was me. I done it."

* * * *

Sheriff Cummings rarely got such a surprising admission of guilt so soon after a crime was committed. He didn't require assistance in arresting the now apparently subdued mild mannered Alex, but McKinney proceeded to affix handcuffs anyway. By now, Lewis and Pleas Largent edged up to the lawmen and the man clothed in the faded overalls, wearing his age evident billed cap, secured in hand cuffs. Lewis called to the arresting officers, "Excuse me, but when can we talk to Mister Tarpin?"

Recognizing the editor, the Sheriff answered, "Call me at the Court House Francis, and I'll let you know." He then led the prisoner to his county car in which they departed for the main highway on the west edge of town. Left remaining on the now glistening wet main street, were a handful of stunned townspeople who began drifting away for shelter.

Three days later, after at least two calls a day to the court house, Francis Lewis finally was able to talk to the sheriff. By then, an outline of the story had come out in the newspaper published in the county seat. But at that point there was nothing printed concerning the motive for the shooting. It was reported, and Sheriff Cummings verified that Tarpin had used his old 22 caliber rifle. Apparently, he marched purposefully the two blocks from his home to the blacksmith shop, confronted Lamis Sagerson in some manner and shot him. There was nothing said in the newspaper nor in the conversation with the sheriff to indicate animosity or revenge as a motive for the shooting.

However, Lewis and all the other fox hunters in town and in the area instantly knew that a person with a compulsive mind committed the act...thus compounding small tragedies into a larger one. Pleas Largent, Colin Bracken and Harry Fielding all knew of the revenge motive possessed by Alex even before he lost his last foxhound.

As far as they knew, Alex had not asked to be provided with a legal counsel so Pleas Largent got in touch with a relative in the County Seat to represent the morose prisoner. At about that time Lewis received permission from the authorities for Largent and Lewis to have a conference with Tarpin. On the appointed day, Lewis picked up Pleas and they drove to the city, neither man possessed with sanguine thoughts regarding the future of their fellow foxhunter.

On that day, late in March, again it was misting rain, low clouds cast a gloomy aura as the two men drove the fifteen miles to the court house. It took another hour for the credentials to be provided and a physical search made by the officers and presiding clerks so that the two visitors might be admitted to the jail cell. They examined carefully the package of cookies Nellie Lewis had sent to the prisoner. The visitors found Alex, still in his overalls seated on the lone cot in the confined place. He looked up when the jailer opened the barred gate, announcing that he had visitors.

Then standing, Alex Tarpin extended his hand to one than the other as he greeted the two men from Portageville. "Howdy do. Mister Lew and Pleas. Sorry to bring this all down on our town." The two visitors patted him comradely on the back and shoulder, and tried to console him. Since they were not allowed by the head jailer to spend more than a few minutes with the prisoner no chairs were provided, which irritated Lewis "Mister Lewis I was so dadburned mad at that Sagerson guy, I lost my head and decided to go after him. He killed all my hounds. Every darn one of them. He deserved what I gave him, don't you know?"

"Have you seen your lawyer?" this from Pleas. Alex nodded and half turned away. Pleas continued, "Does the lawyer know what precipitated this shooting? Seems to me those are mitigating circumstances and a judge ought to go easier with you."

"Well, no matter what, I suppose I'll be goin' away before long. But I just want to say I sure do appreciate you all comin' up here. There wasn't much else to say by anyone as the officer came to dismiss the visitors. They said their goodbys and left.

Before the actual trial took place Tarpin's lawyer had provided an investigator to determine if Sagerson had actually acquired the poison and had administered it…seems that there was evidence that the smithy still had possession of arsenate of lead on a top shelf of the shop. Also wrapped nearby was some stale, rank, ground beef. Since the shop was almost on a direct line from the timber on the north to the Tarpin house down by the creek, it seemed feasible that a foxhound bound for home could be dissuaded from its course and consume the poisoned meat on the way. Thus, the fox hunters and most of the folks in Portageville hoped that these circumstances would save Alex from the Electric Chair.

* * * *

The trial took place in the court room of the county court house. It lasted only two days, conducted before a judge and jury. The verdict for the capital offense was not death, the verdict quietly applauded by the locals, as some people in Portageville had feared the worst, but the jury advised a much lighter sentence of 15 years in the State Penitentiary in Jefferson City. A relieved Francis Lewis had another opportunity to visit briefly with Alex before he was taken the two hundred miles or so to Jefferson City to be incarcerated. At this meeting, Lewis again accompanied by Pleas Largent, asked if there should be anything he might want or wished for at this time.

"Mister Lew and Pleas," now there was no rancor in the voice "I know I did somethin' bad and I have been thinking about it and hopin' that the Lord takes pity on me. But as terrible as my crime was it ain 't as bad as that man a- killin' our hounds. Now, what do l need? he paused a few seconds "I 'spect they will give me 'bout all I need down there But Mister Lewis, I sure would appreciate your continuing to send to me my monthly copy of *The Red Ranger*."

The editor smiled, shook his hand, lightly clapped his other hand on the now gaunt man's shoulder, and told Alex Tarpin that his wish will be fulfilled. "You will get your copy as long as you need it down there. Good luck, Alex."

* * * *

Francis Lewis, this time a passenger in his friend, Pleas Largent's, car remained mostly silent on the ride back to

Portageville, as the sun sank behind the Kansas bluffs to the west.

Lewis pressed his spine into the seat back, turned to Largent and said, "Not much wind and just enough moisture on the ground." Pleas glanced at Lew, grinned, nodded his head and said, "My hounds are ready. Shall we say in about an hour we can head up there on foot into the Maybry Woods? That old reliable "Dog Fox" up yonder is probably rarin' to go too."

Lewis nodded, "Meet me at my place…Nellie is sure to have the coffee on."

* * * *

TISH

Though not without some doubt, I am nevertheless rather certain that my age was fifteen when I first went to work for the laird of Dollar Glen Castle. That was the age which I could best calculate and which I gave to Brother Matthew who became my mentor when he first called at the Workhouse. I have no memory of my parents or kin. It was Brother Matthew, the Cistercian monk, who provided me, who was called simply, Tish, with the opportunity to be rescued from that ugly Workhouse in the city of Perth.

Looking back to those times, I can truly assess the degrading environment of that place into which I was cast at a very early age. In those days, that institution collected the human refuse that authorities prohibited from coexisting with even ordinary folk in the outside world. The borderline criminal, the debauched and even orphans like me all populated a Workhouse. That memory provides me with unbounded joy at having been hired, with Brother Matthew's blessing, by Sir Benjamin Loudon, Viscount and laird of a vast holding based at Dollar Glen Castle, ancient headquarters of the Campbell

Clan, in the mid highlands of Scotland. The year of my arrival and acceptance at the castle, I shall never forget: 1830. It was a Thursday in the spring of that year. I was hired as an apprentice housemaid on a *trial basis*,(according to Brother Matthew.)

The entire castle staff, especially the head housekeeper, Missus Hamilton and her assistant, the pretty Missus Jane Ann Balnaves seemed to like my work and all. But my size may have been another reason they took to me as I was really not very big. 'Tis true indeed, even in my thirties, I was sometimes mistaken for a child. Looking back to my appearance in those early days, I must have been less than impressive with my oat- straw colored hair, large round blue eyes set in a moon face sprinkled with freckles. With the passage of time, I did grow a bit, managed to control my hair, and my body eventually became mature. Missus Jane Ann even began calling me a "pretty lass." Also, I was always strong so that I could do my part at the often strenuous tasks as a maid in that wonderful Dollar Glen Castle.

Sir Benjamin had a wife who lived in the village of Auldonia with two daughters, the wife, Katrina, chose not to live in the castle for reasons only she could reveal. A son, Robert Loudon, was serving in the English King's army when I first arrived at Dollar Glen Castle.

During that first year, when all the Balnaves family lived and worked at the castle, I must say it was the most rewarding time of my life up to then. I won't go into detail describing the unusual circumstances of why all the Balnaves people were living and working for Sir Benjamin. However, I will say that their croft house accidentally burned and the father tragically died in the fire. Since the croft was on part of Sir Benjamin's Campbell holding, the Balneaves survivors sought to pay the balance of the rent they assumed to have owed. It is a long story but suffice it to say they were all given shelter and succor *by* the laird in the castle, and generously given responsible jobs *for* the laird. As I have said.Missus Jane Ann, the mama, assisted Missus Hamilton, the housekeeper. Beautiful Jean and her tall, intelligent brother William, worked in the castle office. Sheila and Mairi did housemaid work and odd jobs, as with me. Fact is, we were *all* much like a big family.

When I joined the staff at the castle, I could not write or read much and could barely express myself with words. That is when Missus Jane Ann took the time to teach me how to read, write and speak. Early on I had adopted the native Scottish terms, words and generic accent of certain classes, folkways that had been adopted by generations of honest hard working Scots. Slowly, I began to possess the terminology in speaking, of a better educated lass, learning the parts of speech and all. Though for months after that year, and even much later, my talk would occasionally lapse into the use of "be" for the English words "am or are." My goodness, I recall Sir Benjamin himself when he was passionate about something, would resort to "ye" for you and even use my old favorite, "be" for is, am or are.

Finally, you must know that another tragedy befell the Balneaves in October of the year I came to the castle. The youngest bairn, Mairi, a lass of about my age slipped and fell from way up on the roof where she and Johnnie, a grandson of Missus Hamilton were attempting to reach one of the towers. She dropped sharply down all the way to the courtyard, sadly losing her life. I missed her terribly as we were both becoming good friends. Afterward, I counted it my duty to comfort Mairi's mama, Missus Jane Ann who was, of course, especially sorely bereaved.

So by the time Jean and Will moved out all the way over to Auchenblae, a town in Kincardinshire at the beginning of the next year, I had received a thorough education at the knee of Missus Jane Ann at Dollar Glen Castle. (Meanwhile, Jean and Will would be helping a linen mill entrepreneur start up back East.)

An important part of my background with the Loudon and Balneaves families is the story of the love affair between Jean Balneaves and Sir Benjamin's only son, Robert. They met each other, I understand, while no more than bairns when Sir Benjamin and young Robert who were on a hunt for wild game just happened onto the Balnaves croft. Years later, Jean and Robert would meet secretly at that remote croft and soon fell in love, much to the consternation of his eccentric mother, Katrine. Soon after, Robert was encouraged to attend a new army Officer's Candidate School in England. The couple remained apart for almost five years postponing their eventual rejoining. Being prohibited from being wedded by an unreasonable Katrine, after Robert was discharged, the couple lived for a time together in Auchenblae anyway.

I was soon ordained to be a part of their lives more directly when in time Jean gave birth to a handsome boy bairn, who was christened David Benjamin Loudon. For that was when Sir Benjamin and Jane Ann gave their blessing to my traveling all the way to Auchenblae to make my home there with Jean and young David. Meanwhile, Robert, by then a major in the Reserve, was recalled to the army. David at that time was an active young lad, who as an adult began his university education. So the low point of our existence happened when our dear Robert perished of a malady on board a ship bound for war in the Crimea. Both mother Jean and David needed my presence more than ever at that time.

Before we skip ahead in time, I must say one of the happiest and deepest honors I have ever received was the day that Jean announced to me that after all those years, I would now possess a surname. No longer would I be addressed simply as "Tish"...from now on I would be "Tish Balneaves." Believe me, I danced around that house for quite a spell alternately hugging Miss Jean and singing to the world... "Tish BALNEAVES, Tish BALNEAVES !"

* * * *

It is a matter of record, I understand, that the people of Scotland experience more than their share of life's struggles. For example, that marvelous old Dollar Glen Castle, headquarters of Sir Benjamin's lairdship, went into decay when much of the holding was lost to unscrupulous dealers.

In Auchenblae, our Jean and Will who were helping the owner, David Hagil, build his growing linen factory saw it go up in an inexplicable mass of flames. The owner lost his life in an attempt to control the fire. In the aftermath, Jean and Will helped the townsfolk to recover from the loss of their livelihood by fairly distributing available funds. Young David was at University at the time where he later earned a Law Certificate. Along about then Will married a nice girl, Maddy, who within a year was with child. Events began moving fast as David became so frustrated in the practice of law in our small town that he decided to emigrate to North America. His mother, my dearest friend, Jean, chose to make the trip with him. That was just last year, 1867... it was also the year I celebrated my fifty second birthday. You must know that I was deeply saddened at the thought of seeing the departure of two people whom I considered family. My spirits lifted when I learned that Will and Will's wife Maddy invited me to live with their family. Being available to help with the approaching birth of a baby bairn was joyfully anticipated.

Nevertheless, saying goodby that September to Jean and David brought forth tears from nearly all who were assembled at the coach stop. So now, I thought, my new life begins.

*   *   *   *

It was a blessing, I felt, living with Will and Maddy Balneaves there in our village of Auchenblae. Caring for little Jean Ann gave me immense joy as she was such a pleasant, delightful bairn. Everyone made me feel as if I were blood kin of the family. Maddy and I would go to market together trundling Jean Ann in her pram that Will had cleverly fashioned. You see before Missus Jean and David had departed, Will had opened up a kind of repair shop which soon became successful. On Sunday's we all attended the Kirk up on the hill across the burn. Will and Maddy had inherited from David Hagil a fine, much larger house over closer to the Kirk, so on Sundays, the trek was easy to make on foot.

Aye, 'twas a good life for me and my Balneaves family. It was around the time of baby Jean Ann's third birthday that my world took another turn. It was the fall of 1868 when *he* rode in to our Auchenblae village. "He" was an apparent stranger who arrived driving a beautiful matched pair of horses pulling a good looking, rather fancy carriage. I can describe this event correctly because I was at William's shop, having been there to fill in at the counter for Maddy.

After jumping down from the driver seat on the open carriage, and looping the reins around a hitching rail out front, the stranger came to the outdoor counter where I was standing. Doffing his riding bonnet he revealed a full head of gray-white hair atop a weathered face adorned by a mustache the color of his hair. "Good afternoon, Madam" he said. "I am presently in need of some repair work on one of my carriage wheels out yonder" as his hand directed my gaze to the high street out front. As an after thought he added, "I rented the carriage, team and all at the Edinburgh Rail Station."

I brushed a wisp of hair away from my face and responded, "Mister Balneaves is back in the shop. Please rest on that chair and I shall fetch him." I don't know why I felt flustered and so unsure … But I excused myself and wiggled around a small table almost blocking my progress as I made for the entrance to the repair shop. At the last moment I halted and asked over me shoulder, "Sir, what *be* your name?"

The stranger grinned, revealing the whitest, nicest teeth, "Madison. Jack Madison… from down London way." The front counter was separated from the shop by a long piece of canvas that served as a door. When I clumsily escaped from the customer around the canvas, I stopped, stood stalk- still placing the palm of my hand to my forehead in pure disgust at my behavior. There I was reverting to my old favorite verb, "be." After clearing my throat, I called out across the shop, "Mister Will, could you come up front please? Ye have a customer who needs help." Will glanced at me as he approached the doorway, wiping his hands with a rag. "You all right Tish? Yer face is carryin' a bit of a glow." I simply nodded aye.

Knowing full well that I was an adult woman, though hardly with nary a trace of sophistication, I nevertheless remained rooted there in mild embarrassment behind the sanctuary of the canvas "door." Soon it all began to flood back in my memory of the man Jack Madison. Then I heard bits and pieces of the conversation between Will and that handsome older mon.

"I say, Mister Will, is it? Can you give me any information about the family of my old friend Robert Loudon? We served in the army together many years ago. I understand he lost his life during the Crimean Unpleasantness. He left behind a son and the son's mother, I believe."

Will paused for an instant from lubricating a carriage wheel hub, straightened up and looked closely at the visitor, replied, first wiping his hand then offering it to shake. "Aye, now I know ye. They shook hands, both smiling I noticed as I peeked around the edge of the canvas doorway. "When things went bad for land owners and all hereabouts, ye kindly and honestly stepped in and helped our families recover their lives. Och, and my name is William Balneaves, as ye might have guessed since this is me shop. Ye be askin' about me Nephew, David and me sister Jean. Then still hidden, I heard Will say, "I warrant that our Tish." then louder, "Tish, come out and properly greet Mister Jack Madison…you must remember him from when he journeyed here some twenty year' ago."

Now I remembered. Jack Madison came to Kincardin-shire on two occasions. Once he called on Sir Benjamin at the castle then later here in Auchenblae after he got word that Mister Robert had died. The last time here he called on Jean. But Miss Jean remained loyally smitten with the memory of Robert as I recall. So I remained in the background though I thought he was a grand mon and quite elegant with his funny, English way of speakin'.

Anyway I emerged from hiding after I dried my hands by smoothing me shop apron. Stepping forward I tried to carry myself erectly as tall as I could manage. Then with some semblance of dignity I offered my hand to Jack Madison who gave me a slight bow, as he took my hand in his. "Indeed I do remember you Miss Tish" he said with an illuminating smile that also made his outstanding eyes crinkle at the edges, "I recall you were a favorite of Robert and Jean. I must say, the years have been most kind to you"

"Thankee, Mister Jack" I finally croaked, glancing away.

"Please, can we dispense with formality in addressing each other. Why can't we be simply...I say, why not Jack and Tish?" Well, let me tell you, my insides began to flutter and it seemed that I would melt into the ground right there between Jack Madison and our Will Balneaves.

Within minutes the faulty wheel hub had been fixed. After paying Will the few coins charged, the men shook hands and bid each other good day. Jack then prepared to again board the carriage but halted in mid effort, looking back at me he spoke. "It would please and honor me, Tish, if you would join me at supper this day. What say you? I could call on you at your lodging."

Before answering, I glanced at Will. See, I lived in his home with Maddy and Jean Ann.he gave a perceptible nod. Then, out of my mouth came, "Certainly. What time of day would that be?" Talk about being shamelessly forward! But I said what I said, as if I were accustomed to being asked out by gentlemen.

Jack Madison replied with that fetching smile, "Smashing, Tish, Shall we say half past six? Very well, I shall see you then...Oh yes, you do live in the Balnaves house on Burnmouth Road, right?"

At that point an obviously bemused William Balneaves, bless his heart, supplied Jack with the directions to cross the burn to find our place on the side of the hillock there.

With a wave and a shout back to me as he drove off, "I have a room at the King David Inn up high street from here. Cheerio."

Armed with a head full of things to know when a gentleman comes a calling, I hurried home, being dismissed early by Will. After all, by then I was over fifty years old and had been privy to courting taking place near and even in my presence. Though my wardrobe was not extensive, I did have two rather important frocks in my possession., used mostly on Sundays, of course. Once I arrived at the house I hurried to my room, chose and laid out the clean clothes on the bed. Just as I was making for the bathroom that William had improved when we moved in a few years ago, Maddy and Jean Ann arrived. I could tell Maddy knew something was up as she offered, "So ye be home early Tish dear?"

Though I was still in something of a dither, I answered Maddy in a voice that didna' betray my excitement one bit. "Oh Maddy, would you believe it, I will be receiving a gentleman caller this eve. A real gentleman."

Then I tilted my head to one side and asked Maddy, "You must remember Robert's English friend, Jack Madison? Of course you do. Well, he came to Will's shop minutes ago today. He actually asked me to have supper with him this very evening." I prattled on, as I looked steadily into Maddy's eyes, "Now why do ye suppose a rich, handsome mon from London would be interested in some low-born Scottish lass like me?"

Maddy is so nice, and figures out people, often without even seeing them, 'cause she put both arms around my shoulders, kissed my cheek and in a gentle voice in her distinctive Scottish burr replied, "Tish, Tish for years ye have been so preoccupied with takin' care of everyone else in this family that ye haven't stopped to get a good look at yourself." Then she released me and led me to the tall mirror in the far hallway. "Tish dear, in that looking glass you see a bonny lass who, if ye never noticed, gets admiring glances from everyone who knows you. And aye, tis a fact, that includes men of all ages too, especially when ye smile." Maddy continued, "Ye have the best eyes and prettiest hair in this part of Scotland. And if ye fit yourself in the right clothes ye would show off in a demure way your very nice, petite figure. So, be yeself, sweet Tish. Whoever asks you to supper...even Mister Jack Madison, will be a fortunate mon." Then, with my face again turning a ruddy color, she said, "now scoot off and make ye-self even prettier."

Just before I ducked into the bathroom I turned to Maddy down the hall and yelled, "He's old, ye know." Then I closed the door and began to make meself ready for the first big evening of me life.

* * * *

Right on the appointed hour, Jack Madison guided his team up the pebble covered drive directly to the front portico of the Balnaves house. I was at the lounge window looking out when I heard the carriage arriving and saw him leap off rather agilely, adjusting his top hat that reflected the same color as his obviously well tailored dark suit, and advanced to the door...so I beat a quick retreat from my station at the window. Maddy, herself, answered the wee bell outside, as she ran through the foyer to the front entrance. I heard her say(and glimpsed her welcoming smile as Jack entered removing his hat in the process...) "Good evening Mister Madison, we are delighted to see ye again. I do believe Tish is in the next room." She raised her voice, "Tish dear, Mister Madison is here." So, I made my entrance, entering the foyer rather too quickly, I fear Anyway, Jack immediately charmed me with a compliment."Well, I dare say Miss Tish you look a vision, truly a veritable vision."

You see, with Maddy's help, we quickly redesigned one

of my frocks so that it was not too flashy but well fitted. As Maddy stitched she had said the garment would be one that seemed to show off my best features for that evening. It was a midnight blue rayon accented with a yellow sash joined by a silver buckle in front. Though they would not show below the hem of my gown, I was wearing the latest (I understand) borrowed rayon knee-length stockings. Draped over one arm was the black velvet cloak Mister Robert chose for me during those months in London with Jack Madison, years ago. I rarely wore it and kept it preserved in a case, I suppose for just such an event as this very occasion. I managed a response, "Thank you kind sir. Ye look most grand I must say." And so we made our exit after we collected our head covers. Maddy had loaned me her clever tam decorated in front with the silver royal thistle of Scotland.

Somehow it seemed easy and natural for Jack to gently help me step into the carriage seat, as he followed me with one hand holding the reins in the driving position. We looked into each other's eyes and laughed gaily. I don't really know what stimulated that emotion in me. Nervousness, perhaps. I only know right then I felt somehow, protected. Special. As if for the first time in my life I was beginning to experience a romantic interlude. Jack Madison spoke first as the horses trotted out to the road leading to the village high street. "I hope, Tish that you will approve of my choice for supper. I recall that the King David Inn served meals the last time I was in Auchenblae."

Of course, I gave him my best smile and nodded vigorously, "Oh aye, that will be guid."

As we moved swiftly along Jack paid attention to the driving but he indicated a genuine curiosity about Jean and David Loudon. There was much I could recall so when we arrived at the dining room, I was prepared to fill in the gaps in Jack's memory regarding their departure and their eventual emigration to America.

After we were seated in the dining room of the Inn, Jack ordered a small bottle of wine. Aye, of course in the living of my life among the Loudons and Balnaves I had tasted certain spirits when there was cause for celebrating some event in our lives. So I relaxed and proceeded to review for Jack the departure from Scotland of Jack's friend David Loudon and his mama Jean. After a long coach ride to the port of Greenock near Glasgow they had boarded a steamship for North America. They eventually found an agreeable place to live in a place called Saint Joseph, Missouri, in the United States of America. Both Sir Benjamin (David's grandfather) and his grandmother Jane Ann are gone now, partially because they were still grieving for Robert...and from David and Jean's departure. I concluded this brief synopsis by wiping a tear So I ventured a smile and let Jack begin a review of his early association with Scotland and our people.

He reminded me that he and Robert Loudon were in the same class at Sandhurst Military School back in 1826. Years later after both Robert and Jack were out of the British Army, Robert came to London on Dollar Glen Castle business. When Jack found he was in the city, he insisted that Robert lodge in the large Madison town house where only Jack and his father, Lord Madison and a butler lived. Jack was unmarried since his betrothed had years ago fled the city with a titled gentlemen from the west of England While Robert was staying there, a tragedy occurred when thieves broke-in the town house, resulting in the brutal bludgeoning to death of the old, faithful Madison butler. At this point in the retelling, the memory of that time caused a frown on the broad forehead. "Sorry," he said as he took another sip of wine. Continuing the recollection, and now looking directly into my eyes, "Robert was scheduled to return to Scotland but because of his help in solving the murder case, he continued his stay at our place, so we became very well acquainted."

"Perhaps you may ask what brings me to this part of Scotland. On the surface, one may suggest that the fact that I have made it my profession to manage investments and land holdings, that logically would bring me to your country. And that would be true enough. However, Tish, I am also a sentimentalist, I confess. My sojourns into the Highlands years ago brought me in contact with the rarest of commodities in life, honest, ethical and honorable Scots. I shall always remember that race of people who provided me with fondly remembered moments in my life that are forever etched into my consciousness. And now, Tish, I have rediscovered you."

Before I could respond to this unexpected and affectionate praise of my Balneaves-Loudon folk, and *me*...the server appeared at our table. Jack Madison, not missing a beat, suggested that if the joint of beef is recommended then looking across to me, "and if my companion agrees, we shall each order that dish. Do you approve Miss Tish?"

I nodded aye, and offered what I hoped would be an adoring smile. As Jack continued to comment on the food, between mouthfuls he would elevate his gaze so that our eyes would lock and hold for an instant. My mind continued to struggle with...what was the word used by Laird Benjamin, aye, *anomaly*, a sort of conflict between my background and Jack Madison's. But I listened closely as Jack revealed his innermost thoughts and I almost had to pinch myself to know this was not a wanton dream. Jack's words and gestures were lavished on me, about whom he had no romantic thoughts as recently as this very morning.

Finally, as he laid down his knife Jack folded his napkin and looked again at me sitting bolt upright across from him. "Tish, forgive me, but allow me to guess your age. I would think your age might be, what? Going on forty or so?"

I swallowed and said, "Jack, I be, I *am* fifty three this year."as I again found his expressive eyes that thankfully didna' betray an ounce of disappointment. He almost leaped out of his chair "I say Tish, splendid. That puts us squarely in the same generation. On my birthday this year I shall be fifty nine years old." Ignoring the other two couples in the dining room, Jack stood and helped me to a standing position and held me in an almost suffocating hug with my face in his cravat and his lips in my hair. Shortly, still grinning he paid the server for the meal and led me outside.

What transpired over the next few hours was the beginning of a familiarity that I had never known. Jack Madison was a head taller than I but as we walked along the high street of Auchenblae that evening, a casual viewer might see one figure moving slowly in the semi-darkness, with barely audible voice sounds emanating therefrom. I freely admit, as I have earlier in my story, that my sudden liaison with a man, any man was totally unexpected. Yet I must say that perhaps the Lord God played a part in this wonderful new experience. Being at Will Balneave's shop this very morning was the beginning of it all. Within the hour we were back in Jack's carriage as the team used a slower pace back to my lodging at Will and Maddys. At the door, as I had secretly hoped, Jack tilted my head back, leaned down and kissed me fervently. Of course, it was my first ever kiss from a lover and I rejoiced, kissing him back with lingering passion. Finally, he bid me goodnight."May I see you tomorrow, Tish dear? I have a couple of chaps to see early on the morrow, may I return here by the noon hour?" My answer was a final kiss and a vigorous nod that sent my blood a racin' and poundin'.

Jack Madison remained in Auchenblae for nine days more. We spent time together almost constantly at tea, dinner and late evening coffee. The first few days he would renew his acquaintance with our town and the various shops and the bank along high street and beyond. Often we were given space at the Balnaves' house. Other times we were at tea rooms or pubs in the village. Then there was the day before the dreaded departure date. Which, of course meant Jack Madison would be returning to Edinburgh and eventually to London. That evening Jack was invited to join Will, Maddy, little Jean Ann and me at our house. And it was that very evening before we seated ourselves at table, that Jack became very quiet and his face revealed a serious intensity that I was unaccustomed to seeing in our relatively brief courtship.

Sitting next to me on the settee in the formal hearth room, he leaned away from me, reaching into his vest and withdrew a small box. "Sweet Tish," he whispered, "In my lifetime I have met and courted ladies of various levels in society and they have fallen short in my appraisal, I must admit. Frankly I had come to believe that a special person did not exist that would capture my heart as you have done. The qualities you possess have brought me to this most wonderful conclusion. Dearest Tish, will you consent to be my wife and reside with me in London?"

With Jack's emotional declaration, I must admit to having at first been frozen in place as my heart began to pound furiously in my breast. Placing one hand over my chest and with the other stretched out to touch Jack Madison's face…well, I must tell you I wept! Tears of unrestrained joy, I suppose, as Jack then presented me with the contents of the fancy box.

"Tish, after that first evening, I found the silversmith in town who fashioned this according to my instructions. It is not yet completed but I wanted you to see it tonight." Then he handed me the box which I nervously opened. Inside was an obviously high quality silver piece gorgeously fashioned into a stylized letter 'T'. Jack hastened to add, "If you will say 'yes', to my proposal, love, we shall in London have diamonds set along the entire surface of the brooch, this "T for Tish", as many as will fit."

My head was in a whirl. But I have to say I said aye, before Jack came to his senses and withdrew the proposal. Then we hugged as the other Balneaves came into the hearth room'

"My but we had a glorious party in that house that evening. Will and Maddy were effusive in their congratulations, pouring out their love to me in their affectionate embraces, kisses and hugs. Even little Jean Ann danced around the house, not realizing I am sure, that I would soon be departing her house. In fact, Jack had to delay our departure another full day and both he and I had numerous tasks to perform before we loaded up the carriage for Edinburgh and London. First Jack had to arrange for passage on the trains out of Edinburgh for both of us this time, using the new telegraph in town. Then I was obligated to acquire an appropriately tasteful traveling wardrobe for my new life, realizing with Maddy's advice that the most wonderful shops lay in my future in London Town. Also, Jack had some business matters to wind up with some important people in the area. But most importantly, we had an hour reserved with the Reverend John Cooks of the parish kirk. So I was so proud to be wed to my Jack Madison in the same kirk in which David Loudon, son of Robert Loudon and Jean Balnaves were baptized back in 1832. Before the ceremony I asked the aging pastor to show us the notation in the rolls indicating that the baptismal ceremony had included both parents and "others" which included grandparents Laird Benjamin Loudon and Jane Ann Balneaves.

And then we were wed! Such happiness I had never imagined in my most fanciful dreams. As we left the kirk, Jack and I held each other close and walked down to Will and Maddy's house as if we were one person. Within the hour Mister and Missus Jack Madison had said their repeated farewells to Will and Maddy and little Jean Ann. Amid tears all around, we finally boarded the carriage loaded with our belongings and away we drove. Our first stop would be an Inn in the city of Dundee which we reached just as the sun sank below the Highland hills. And there Jack and I spent our first night as mon and wife.

* * * *

The next day, amazingly, Jack remembered the Inn on Princes Street in Edinburgh where years earlier, Robert Loudon had spent the night after leaving the army on his return to Scotland. So that is where Jack and I spent our second night together. For us both we were enraptured with the experiences we shared. Afterward I sobbed a little knowing how fortunate I was, a mere waif as a child, to have a well bred wonderful husband this late in life.

Though we were older than most wedded couples, we couldn't have been happier. I will admit that my head and body were filled with the thrills and wonder of the wedding bed, and the sights and sounds during the days that followed almost overwhelmed me. The ancient city of Edinburgh was sampled the next day. But the amazing ride on the train to London was never to be forgotten. Jack, of course, was most sweet and understanding of my big eyed look at the world that I had never seen before. When the time came for us to leave the train at the noisy rail station in London, I did grasp Jack's hand firmly as he saw to the transfer of our baggage to one of the numerous horse drawn hacks. In an excited voice, Jack said, "Wait 'til you see our house, Tish. It is located right in the center of London. I am sure my telegram reached my, (I must remember to say OUR) butler Smythe, so he will be expecting us. My father, Lord John Madison passed away more than ten years ago, as you know but Smythe came to us earlier after we lost dear old Cranmer."

I could only nod and keep a smile on my face as I tried to file all these facts away in my mind. Finally, the hack stopped before an impressive multistory house. Before Jack could ring the bell, a formally dressed man about Jack's age showing a broad smile stepped nimbly down the steps to grasp Jack's hand, "Welcome home Mister Jack. And my, this lovely creature is our Missus Madison?"

"You are quite right Smythe. Can you manage the cases there, perhaps the driver will assist you." So we entered the most impressive house I have ever seen since Dollar Glen Castle in the old days. It had to be rather more ornate than the wonderful Andrew Macdill manor house in Dundee that Jean, Robert and others had admired and raved about.

Over the next ten days or so, I tried to absorb all that I needed to know to fill my role as the Lady of The House. Getting acquainted with the staff was my first priority. The housekeeper was Irish whose name was Missus Gander who made me feel at home when she laughed a good natured chuckle saying, "Me name's Gander, just like the *he* goose, Madam." I hugged her ample waist and joined her amusement in the little gibe at her own expense. There were two younger house boys and three part time housemaids that aided the higher ranking servants; and finally our full time cook who was rather large, rosy cheeked and a bit jolly, named Audrey. I immediately liked them all and pledged to myself to be a responsible, caring Lady of The House. But mainly I moved through the days following as if I were in a fairyland as Jack made sure that my every wish should be granted, even though I knew not enough to express a wish for anything more than a life with Jack Madison.

Once we were settled and in possession of paper and ink, I felt an urgent need to write to my family back in Scotland. There was a rather private area off our bedroom that contained a desk, writing paper and pen and ink. I addressed and wrote the letter as follows:

From Tish Balneaves Madison
Madison Town House
Barckley Square
London England
To William, Maddy and Jean Ann Balneaves
Balneaves House,
Auchenblae
Scotland

Dearest Maddy, William and Jean Ann

Jack and I have had the most interesting experiences traveling to London. I have seen sights that I never ever dreamed of. Though we did not spend much time in Edinburgh on the way, I know enough of our history to want some day to really explore that ancient city.

But the real treat is this massive house here in London. We are located on one of the prettiest and busiest squares in the city, Jack says. I have only begun to explore the various floors and rooms.

Our room, (Jack's and Mine) is decorated nicely but a bit on the masculine side which I don't mind a bit, but Jack just this morning suggested that I get with Missus Gander, the housekeeper, and do with it as we wish. Jack is such a dear man, I can't believe everything that has happened to me in the past month. Heaven must have opened up and deposited dear Jack at my feet. Thanks be to God.

I shall try to keep in touch. Meanwhile, write when you can and tell me all the news. We love you all.

Tish

October 17, 1868

Within days of our arrival in London Jack took my silver brooch as he left for his office. He had found the skilled artisan who set the entire piece with perfect small diamonds. When he brought it home a few days later I must say it was dazzling...not flashy, but simply a work of art. I am so proud of it that I wear it above my heart even around the house; of course whenever we venture out into the city I wear it with pride, knowing that my *"T for Tish"* is my most precious inanimate possession.

* * * *

The succeeding years were very good and rewarding to both Jack and me. Honestly, there were days when I had to concentrate my mind to realize that I once lived in Auchenblae and at Dollar Glen Castle. The Madison Town House staff continued to be most efficient. The redecorating of our room early on met with my mon's enthusiastic approval, as were the few other touches Missus Gander and I dreamed up. I so looked forward to the time of day when Jack would return home from the office. We would often sit in our large front room close to each other and discuss his day, which now included sessions in parliament's House of Lords. Jack had finally succeeded his honored father. He was officially now, Lord John Madison. The obvious condition of this elevated status was that I was expected to join Jack at certain receptions and the occasional ball. Jack, in the course of time had shown his age only by seeing his hair and mustache turn almost totally white. While my light colored hair had only barely faded somewhat. He would joke that he was fortunate that his wife still loved him as an old man.

Believe me when I say that I seemed to fit at the parties and receptions. Few, if any, in our social world knew of my "low" birth. As far as they knew I was plucked by t he Loudons and Balneaves from under a gooseberry bush. We were able to travel abroad to the continent when business or government needs demanded. All of which served to broaden my knowledge and sensory experiences of our world. I fervently hoped that we would find a reason to visit again my homeland in Scotland one day. Often we would promise ourselves that this would happen but the years seem to happily glide past and we had yet to wend our way north.

It was the ninth of October in the year 1878, ten years from the date we were wed that my world crashed about me. Missus Gander and I were discussing a different arrangement of the furniture in the receiving room. It was nearly eleven on the clock when we heard the protracted jangling of the bell at the entrance door. Gander hurried to answer since Smythe was in another part of the house.

Gander opened the door as I observed from some distance away. Before her was a uniformed gentleman, breathless, asking "Is Lady Madison here, please. I have terrible news. O'im constable Darnell. Please…" as I walked toward the doorway on trembling legs, the policeman continued when he saw that I was present, "Excuse me yer ladyship, but Lord Madison has been gravely injured."

His words seemed foreign to me as I attempted to respond but I was unable to form audible sounds as my throat seemed suddenly dry and lifeless. Nevertheless with Gander's help and with a nod from me, we invited the constable into the near room. After he first removed his helmet we three, seated ourselves. Missus Gander softly asked, "Where sir may her ladyship go to see Master Jack?" "His lordship was taken to hospital, madam, that be all I kin say. 'Bout all Oi know is that it happened suddenly,an accident it were. So sorry Yer Ladyship." The disconnected conversation was terminated by another jangle of the bell out front. I jumped at the sound. At the door this time was one of Jack's secretary s, I believe it was Henry Brashear who hurried to us seated there, halted an arm's length away, bare headed and bowed to me as he reported that my dear Jack was gone. Dead he was, and my heart stopped for I don't know how long.

Smythe came running down from one of the upper levels, took in the scene and came quickly, tears in his eyes to console me as I sat there trying to come to grips with all this horrible news of the tragic passing of the dear mon, that warm hearted mon who was my love, indeed my life Jack Madison.

It was almost an hour before I learned that while on his way to inspect property, Jack and one of his men prepared to cross a street within walking distance of his office when the accident happened. It is difficult for me to visualize it but Mister Brashear who was accompanying Jack said it was totally capricious what happened. "We had just been watching for traffic before crossing the street when out'a nowhere came this gigantic piece of lumber afallin' off the nearby building under repair. The huge timber grazed my shoulder but caught Lord Madison squarely in back of the head.Oh God, "Mister Brashear sobbed, "ifn only I could have taken it instead. I am sorry your ladyship. I feel so daft"

It took me a little longer to grasp the tragedy, enabling me to bear up and appropriately respond as one should in my present status. But first I must see my husband "Will someone take me to, where? The hospital or the mortuary Thank you all, now one of you with a cart or coach, I should like to see my husband as soon as I can find a wrap. Thank you."

Aye, sad to say, I did finally see my Jack Madison still at hospital but lifeless. I left it to his office staff and the government to take care of the arrangements. I said goodby to my love and prayed a silent prayer for his deliverance and then, asked to be taken back to the Madison Town House.

The time between Jack's accident and the funeral were the worst of times. My rock, my soul, was gone and I was alone. Alone in that massive house. Alone in London town. Instinct told me that I should inform the entire staff that they would be retained, at least in the immediate future. Smythe, Missus Gander, Audrey and all were grateful though continued to mourn their longtime master and friend.

After the state funeral, appropriate for a member of the House of Lords, I began to take stock of myself. Jack's terrible death came in his sixty ninth year. I was near sixty three years of age and suddenly began to feel my age But I learned that I was now a very, very rich widow. Jack owned his business as well as other properties in England and some holdings here and there in Scotland Ah, Scotland, I thought. It has been so long, and I have family there who have been keeping me informed of their lives these past ten years.

On the day Jack's will was processed I learned that except

for a generous sum left to a daughter of his only sister, herself long gone, I was otherwise named the primary inheritor of his estate. The sums mentioned, when converted to pounds sterling, befogged my mind. So it took me weeks to respond to the many messages of condolences as well as making sure that my liquid assets were properly assigned to me by the various banks. But when all those tasks were accomplished my next important step was to turn over the Town House to the people I knew best in London… Smythe,.Missus Gander and Audrey. The younger boys and the housemaids were given grants and dismissed. Now, I was ready to return, though with a heavy heart, to Auchenblae, Scotland. Packing was a bit of a chore but as long as I had my *"T for Tish"* brooch on my dress, I was quite ready to leave my London home.

Preparing the Balneaves house for my arrival required that I use the telegraph this time so that they might meet me at the new train service to Dundee, just a moderate day's carriage ride from Auchenblae. On the train as the rails took me north, I composed a short list of a few of the things I wished to accomplish in Scotland, now that I was a widowed "woman of means."

William, looking quite the same after ten years, had his carriage at the train station in Dundee. Maddy was not quite up to the long drive "both ways" she thought. But Jean Ann, now in her mid teens had accompanied her papa.Will shouted when he saw me step off my coach, "Haloo Tish…over here." I recognized the voice and hastened my pace and fell into his strong arms. Then I cried. And I continued weeping as we walked closer to Jean Ann in the carriage. "I'm sorry Will, I just fell to pieces just now, for the first time really, since Jack…"Then I broke down again. Will held me and stroked my back whispering, Now, now, bonny lass, ye be home.(Precious Will, I was ever the "Young Lass" to him.)

I dried my eyes and blew my nose before I hugged Jean Ann who lovingly responded with a kiss on my cheek and the words I needed to hear, "We missed ye so much, Tish."

The scene was repeated when, late that evening we arrived at the Balneaves house. Maddy and I clung to each other as we both cried, shedding copious tears. Poor Jean Ann joined the weeping as she knew really, that we were also so joyful at being reunited after so many years They had made ready my old room and that is where I lay that night getting my first good rest since I lost my Jack.

Though the Balneaves knew that I must have inherited substantial sums neither one mentioned that thought. It was I who that next morning told them what I had in mind at least for some of the money. I didn't wish to wait any longer. So during breakfast I outlined my thoughts, reading from my notes I had made earlier.

"First, dear ones, I am providing a good portion of the income from the estates for you, Will, Maddy and Jean Ann for as long as ye are alive."

"Secondly, If that dreadful Workhouse in Perth is still operating I will purchase it and turn it into a legitimate school, or college for girls. If it no longer exists, I shall simply build the college anyway.

"Thirdly, I will find the owner of the croft land where our Balneaves family lived years ago and where Will's father lay buried, I intend to buy it, putting it under our Balneaves ownership.

"And Fourth, I intend to take this family, *our* family to America. Of course I am talking about reuniting for a visit with our family that lives in that place in the state of Missouri,

United States of America, where our dear David Loudon and his mama, Jean Balneaves settled, back a few years ago,

I recall the place is named Saint Joseph." After I had announced these plans, there was a momentary pause which was broken by all three Balneaves who stood and gave me yet another loving hug, Maddy and Jean Ann sobbing in the process. Will held me by the shoulders looked down at me with eyes that were damp, said, "Tish, Tish, ye be so special. If only Sir Benjamin and Mama Jane Ann could see confirmed, what a genuine treasure ye are. They would be so proud of you and how ye have managed your life. Thank ye so much, love."Maddy, in turn, offered, as she held my hand, "Will Dear, I be certain that your mama and Sir Benjamin know about Tish right now. I feel it."

This was followed by the namesake of our legendary Jean Balneaves and her mama Jane Ann, saying, "Look mama and papa." Jean Ann looked closely at my diamond decorated silver *"T for Tish"* brooch which, as always, was pinned above my heart. Then in open mouthed wonder, she said, Look at the diamonds on the silver T. That is the most beautiful thing I have ever seen." Jean Ann clapped her hands in admiration. Maddy agreed as both leaned over to get a better look.

I took a sip of coffee, cleared my throat and with a full heart avowed: "If I can no longer have my Jack alive, most certainly I will carry the emblem of our love, my *"T for Tish"* brooch until me dying day. And since I was not blessed with a bairn of my very own, I suspect our Jean Ann will one day wear it in remembrance of her Tish Balneaves Madison."

* * * *

Author's Note

This story contains various names of some of the author's ancestors who lived in Scotland in the nineteenth century. Readers may recognize some of the same characters in my novel, "A Cameo for Jean." In fact this short story might be termed a sequel to that more comprehensive work published in 2003. Two of these forebears emigrated to America, arriving there and actually settling in Missouri during President Grant's Administration. A few names are made up for this fictionalized version of events portrayed here. Our main protagonist, Tish, represents a fusion of various Scottish retainers that are remembered and named by the author's kin, several of whom provided significant reliable anecdotal data used to describe that remarkable, resilient, "bonny lass," Tish.

* * * *

GRACE AND HER AMAZING VIOLIN

Half a normal lifetime ago, the wizened, bearded man bending over his workbench had booked passage on a ship out of the port of Wilhamshaven in the European province of Schleswig Holstein. The vessel's destination was the port city of Osaka on the large island of Honshu, the main island in the nation of Nippon. (Years later, that Asian country would be known as Japan.) He had heard that here, he Gerhard, and other violin makers would be welcomed with open arms. And indeed they did find new homes in cities such as Osaka and Kobe.

Now, he adjusted his spectacles and with both hands lifted from its holding frame, the essence of his recent creation. The instrument before him was the body of a violin, seven days past the last coating of laquer that gave it a glorious red-gold sheen. Herr Gerhard had weeks ago fixed inside the body, certain data including his mark with the declaration that this instrument was made in Nippon. This was a necessity so that the violin's identity would forever be traced to his hands.

So, it was now ready to accept the accouterments familiar

to every violin virtuoso or, perhaps that person newly acquiring the tedious art of making the instrument sing. In preparation, today he would set it aside on a soft cloth within arms reach. Thus he began to assemble the tailpiece, tail adjuster and sound post. He reached for a previously beautifully fashioned wooden bridge and the complete set of four Pro Arte type violin strings with tuning keys. Alongside the already gracefully shaped bow he carefully laid the strands of hair that would be affixed onto that bow. Now he allowed himself a moment of relaxation as he pulled up a stool on which he seated himself, stretched, rested and reflected on the events years ago that brought him to this time and place.

The powerful Chancellor of the recently formed collection of formerly independent Germanic States was named Otto von Bismark. His decree to all under the Prussian King's rule demanded that men of a certain age would be invited, nay forced, to serve in the growing military that was being formed. Our violin maker had chosen, as did many others in that part of the world, to emigrate to safe havens. He had followed the lead of a handful of other violin craftsmen who had braved the long journey by sea to Nippon in the far east. These artisans would be welcomed, even honored. Moreover, the required raw materials such as the variety of woods, surprisingly, the wonderful Carpathian spruce and other components were readily accessible. It was known that an experienced violin maker could carve the delicate neck and scroll.

As he stroked his beard he knew this finished instrument might well find its way to that exciting free, new world the United States of America. For this was the year 1895 as it was known in the Western World when change was everywhere. In his lifetime he had seen and marveled at the advances in science and in everyday life for most of the world. The times were even now being called the Industrial Revolution.

Coincidently, in April of that year, a baby girl was born in the state of Kansas, in America. The infant was named Grace. She was the first born of Agnes Loudon Haines and C. Frank Haines. Frank was truly a versatile individual, handsome and very bright. Though he was working with his wife's father, David Loudon, in the newspaper business, he became a qualified pharmacist. His overriding first love, however, was music, teaching himself to play all the brass and string instruments that existed in those days.

By the time the fifth child was born to this energetic couple, they followed David Loudon to Missouri, settling in the community of Rushville where Frank Haines became engaged in pharmacy. He also prescribed spectacles and helped his father- in- law in the printing business. Very soon, Frank began to assemble band instruments and taught interested residents to play various horns, banjos, and yes, violins. He subsequently formed a city band and became its leader.

Daughter Grace shared her father's affection and proclivity for music. She quickly learned to read music and to play a piano. In her spare time, as a twelve year old, she was fascinated with all the various instruments Frank had acquired. It was most apparent that Grace had aptitude for music at an early age.

At some point shortly before she was thirteen, her father on one of his infrequent shopping visits to the city of Saint Joseph, called on a source who had supplied him with various brass and string instruments. Frank saw, suspended on one wall a violin carrying a color and workmanship that intrigued him. Thinking of Grace, Frank held it in his hands, put it under his chin, then drew the accompanying bow across the strings. The sound was lyrical and he knew that his daughter would love it. As he examined the violin he looked closely through one of the artistic, cleft note -like openings to see the data put there inside the body by the German craftsman in Nippon several years ago.

The dealer could only say the instrument was acquired from an estate being closed in the city. He could furnish little authenticity of the violin. But Frank asked permission to once more hear the sound it could produce. Again, after a perfunctory tuning, he drew the bow across the strings and immediately knew he had to have it. The deal was made to the satisfaction of both parties, which included a battered leather covered case and a spare bow. Thus the transaction was concluded and it was back to Rushville, and home with his treasure.

Grace was astonished and ecstatic when papa presented the gift just before her thirteenth birthday. Indeed it was her most prized possession as she was known to say time and again for months. Though she helped mama take care of her four siblings and worked in the print shop of a locally pub-lished magazine and attended the local school, Grace prac-ticed the violin every spare moment. It soon became evident that she could caress only the clearest, pure tones from those four strings that resonated from the body of the violin.

Four years later Grace fell in love. A tall dignified young man had been summoned from Iowa to take over the posi-tion of editor of that magazine. At a reception for the new editor, the town honored him with a musical concert. Of course, Grace and her violin were featured and even before either knew it she and Lewis, the editor, had fallen in love. They married on Grace's eighteenth birthday, Easter Sunday 1911.

Their first child, a boy, Loudon, named for Grace's Scottish born grandfather, David Loudon, was born in May the following year. Then came Letha three years later. Another son was born named Lee Emerson, after another five years. All this time, Grace practiced and played her violin at home and played in concert at various times around the area. Among her offspring, it was Loudon who had inherited the instinctive gift of music Letha was given music lessons and was able to play the piano. Lee Emerson chose not to bother. Being the youngest he got away with it. Though it was much to his regret later in life when he appreciated the concept and artistry of all musicians.

Loudon took violin lessons from an instructor in St. Joseph. He rapidly became proficient using Grace's very own violin. He also found he had an aptitude for most other musical instruments such as the trumpet as well as most string instruments, as did his Grandfather Haines. However, it was Grace whose music coming from the venerable violin that held the family and many others entranced.

This writer must now admit a tinge of prejudice in this anecdotal story. For I am the third child who can recall the devotion apparent that was felt by my mother, Grace, when she performed. Her unexpected death occurred after a fall in the family home and the failed attempt to repair a damaged pelvic bone...and the resulting pneumonia. Lewis survived her by five years. Loudon had meanwhile died three years earlier after being hospitalized for years following a bazaar auto accident (from which he was faultless.) Letha's family resided on the west coast. So it was I who inherited the amazing violin.

It was cocooned in it's worn leather case for many years... in the family home in Rushville and in the two homes we

have owned in the city of Shenandoah, Iowa. On one occasion several years ago I opened the violin case. I was dismayed
to find the strings awry and the hair on the bow missing
entirely. When I lifted the violin out of the case, I detected a
hairline crack on the body. To this day it is a mystifying thing
that happened…someone or something had caused the once
beautiful instrument to be damaged. I replaced it in the old
case and continued with operating my business, though occasionally possessed by the memory of that violin.

It was spring of the year 2007, having the time, I conducted some research to locate someone with the skills to
renew Grace's violin. I found a source in Omaha, Nebraska
… A. Cavallo Violins, LLC. Phoning the address, I talked
at length with Alex, the principal owner who assured me he
would like to see the instrument. I delivered it immediately
and he eagerly accepted my challenge to rehabilitate the violin
to it's original condition. It would be expensive as Alex would
have to perform some major "surgery." By late fall of 2007 he
phoned to say it was ready. My wife and I drove expectantly
the sixty plus miles to retrieve Grace's violin.

Alex brought forth the instrument and it *was* beautiful
with everything perfect, including the glorious laquer coating. We were most pleased The best bow now accepted the
new hair, as good as the original selected by the violin maker
in Nippon. (For it was Alex who provided me with the story
including the violin's provenance, and of Gerhard, the violin maker.) Tentatively, I asked Alex if he might play a few
chords for us. He smiled, nodded his head and played part of
a violin classic I recognized but could not name. The sound
was vibrant. It was just beautiful! I settled up and placed it
tenderly, again in the original super-stressed leather case for
its trip home.

Though I am not gifted enough to play any violin. Perhaps a grandchild or great grandchild will proudly play and hear its tones. For now, it resides in a handsome bird's eye maple violin stand, atop one end of our piano in our living room. At the base of the stand is a brief statement of its history in our family. Indeed that instrument is one of *my* priceless possessions…Grace's Amazing Violin.

Lisa with her great grandmother Graces's Violin in the year, 2010.

* * * *

Integer Man

Born in rural Atlantic, Iowa in 1879, only fourteen years after the end of America's bloody Civil War, my subject had few of the advantages collected by people of means in that time and that place. It is a fact that he was actually born in a log cabin around which his father later added a frame house. In the nineteen seventies a service club in the city of Atlantic acquired the original logs from that log cabin and erected it once more in an attractive city park in that city, with an accompanying granite memorial to that family.

One of ten siblings produced by a mother whose linage included kinfolk living in Kentucky and Virginia, he also knew two maternal grandparents who emigrated from Scotland. On his father's side were first generation Americans of German descent. The name of this complete man of integrity: Lewis Francis Gingery, whose one lifelong lingering memory of his early childhood concerned an abortive homestead adventure. Fueled by initial optimism the entire family traveled by covered wagon from Western Iowa into the Sand Hills of Nebraska in 1885. The family abandoned the sod house and returned to Iowa exactly one year later, delighting the mother and all the children.

The first record of Lew's complete integrity (or in this case, perhaps his fastidiousness,) can be traced to his early life growing up working on the family farm in Iowa after the Nebraska homesteading fiasco. His father produced various plants for resale. It seems that at every opportunity while working in the fields Lew would hurry to the well pump to wash his hands. When an older brother teased him about this, the father stated that "Every family should have at least one gentleman." During those teenage years while hunting with a brother his shotgun exploded in his face causing him to lose an eye and almost his life.

He did recover, retaining his ambition. The only individual among his siblings who yearned at an early age to improve himself, in Lew's case, by reading the law. Barely out of the teens he mentioned this wish to one of his father's acquaintance in the town of Atlantic, Iowa. Lew was told that there was a law school in Chilicothe, Missouri. He was thrilled with the news, even though he knew that town was more than two hundred miles away. Utilizing most of his meager savings, the young man purchased a ticket that would transport him by passenger train all the way to that town in northern Missouri. Almost immediately, at the conclusion of that long trip, Lew learned that the anticipated college did not exist. One can imagine the bitterness that must have been pervasive on the train ride back home, and the snide remarks by some that he knew would be cast in his direction. But Lew refused to moan about that disappointing experience early in his life. He had too much pride to confront the purveyor of the false information. He simply moved on, acquiring a license to deal in real estate in the neighboring small town of Earlham, Iowa.

He rented a small office that happened to be next door to the local telephone exchange.

A few weeks later as he was sitting at his desk, he heard the operator next door shriek, "*Charlie Barnett's house is on fire!*" Lew ran to the street saw a buggy and team with a driver sitting there. He gave the driver directions to the burning house out on the edge of town. When the swift team of horses brought them to the house it was not completely engulfed with flames though it was burning lively. Suddenly he could hear a child crying. It's parents were apparently hunting for the infant while attempting to escape the fire. Lew rushed into the smoke and flames, swooped up the child who was in the kitchen and retreated while shouting to the parents to exit quickly as he had brought out an infant girl.

The child's parents knew that Lew was a young business-man in that small town of Earlham. They had evidently followed his expanding career. Actually twenty years later he received a letter containing a clipping from a newspaper reporting that Miss Barnett, the pictured young woman, had won a beauty contest in Iowa. The Barnetts wanted Lew to know that the baby he saved had done quite well in life, thanks to his heroic action. This letter was the first his family knew of that brave act.This may be an appropriate place to mention an episode in Lew's youth as reported in a letter he received many years later from his youngest brother, Grover. After the initial amenities, Grover wrote:

"Remember one night in the long ago when we drove your beautiful grey pacing mare to Atlantic and tied up at the corner of Fifth and Walnut Streets? You were around twenty then and I was seven years younger. You tied the filly alongside another single rig owned by a young man from another town. When we started across Walnut Street to go home, the young man who owned the

other rig tied near ours, and two other men, hurriedly got into their buggy and drove away. When we reached our buggy we discovered the lap rug was missing. You were furious, remember? Anyway, instead of driving their route to their home they drove to Third Street, our way home, so we caught up with them in a few blocks and started to drive around, but they whipped up and you had to pull up behind them. You tried again to drive around. One of the men called out 'We dare you to race us Gingery' (they knew your name.) Obviously they were looking for trouble. Well, you answered, 'I can't drive around you…but I think I can whip all three of you !'

We stopped under a street light. It was directly in front of the home of Mrs. Brown, (I think that was her name, a widow of one of the notorious Crooked Creek Gang.) I clearly remember you handing me the lines and stepped to the groun and took off your hat, coat, tie and glasses and put them on the buggy seat; unbuttoned your shirt collar and stood there. Hands at your side with one foot ahead slightly. It is all so clear what happened next when two men got out of their buggy. The larger of the two headed for you first. You stood motionless until he was in reach of you. Then without ceremony you landed a hard right and a left to the man's jaw and he dropped to the ground. His friends helped him back into their buggy and they drove away. I also remember the following day when we drove back into town Mrs. Brown waved us down. She told you she had seen many fights and some killings but had never seen a man as cool in a fight as you were. Remember?"

The above quotation from Lew's brother Grover doesn't mention that Lew was a well developed six footer weighing a compact hundred eighty pounds. Nor is there a record now, more than a hundred years later, if the stolen lap rug was retrieved.

In that rural Iowa neighborhood there was an acquaintance, a young man, a friend whom Lew admired. His surname was Meredith whose destiny that Meredith believed, would take place in the capital city of Des Moines. It is not clear from notes and letters extant whether Lew was invited to accompany Meredith to the city. What is a matter of record is that friend, E.T. Meredith, did find a large measure of success in founding the Meredith Publishing company. The early and lasting success of his properties, Better Homes and Gardens and Successful Farming are testaments to that successful venture. What is evident is that Lew also loved writing and the printed word. Though not possessing higher academic credentials in that rural Iowa area, he did read extensively and was an astute observer. It followed that his abilities in leadership and with the pen preceded him.

Case in point. Around that time, Lew met there in Iowa with a leading citizen of a small community in Missouri. It seems that the visitor was sent to sound him out about his interest in applying for an assistant editor position at a magazine in the town of Rushville, Missouri. It was a new little journal that wonder of wonders, was dedicated to the sport Lew enjoyed, fox hunting. You see, Lew had acquired at an early age two fox hounds of dubious parentage but which would trail a fox "giving mouth" to the sound in the race that Lew learned to love. (It was a humane sport, as the fox would usually go to its den when the sly animal tired of the fun.) Lew always assumed his love for hounds and fox hunting had been inherited from his mother's family who followed the sport back in Kentucky.

So, again, off he went by train to Council Bluffs, thence south to Saint Joseph, Missouri. Eleven miles beyond Saint Joseph the train stopped at a station serving Rushville, a quaint village in the bluffs along the Missouri River. This time Lew was older and more sure of himself, now being almost thirty years of age. With measured confidence the morning after his arrival, Lew walked along main street to the office of The Red Ranger Publishing Company. Though he found, as the negotiations proceeded, that the magazine was losing money every month he could see the possibilities. Therefore, the small group of stockholders and town leaders after interviewing Lew, asked him to accept the job of assistant editor. He accepted but stated that he would have to return to Iowa to settle his affairs there. So the deal was made. The night before he departed, the entire staff, including musicians in the town gave him a parting band concert which he enjoyed very much. He was especially taken with the young, almost eighteen year old lass, an office employee, who played the violin. Her name was Grace.

True to his word, Lew did return to Rushville and took up the duties of the assistant editor of The Red Ranger magazine…so named after the red fox that ranged over the woodland areas throughout America. Slowly but surely the revenues began to rise. So on Christmas Day of that year, 1911, Lew asked Grace Haines' hand in marriage, They were married the following Easter Sunday which was the bride's eighteenth birthday. Grace's parents were pleased with the union as it was obvious Lew's future was indeed bright as he had already been promoted to editor. Soon they began to show a nice profit with subscription and ad revenue actually growing with every issue. Shortly the property became the leader among the three fox hunting journals in America at that time.

One of Lew's favorite hunting companions in the town was Tom Bracken. He was older than Lew and carefree about hygiene as he seemed to carry with him a kind of gamey aura.

But Tom possessed an infectious laugh when amused. More importantly he loved fox hunting Though he sprang from a prominent family he had soon managed to spend his inheritance on drink and ladies of the evening.

But in his middle years Tom eschewed drink and wayward women, doing odd jobs for the townspeople though he really preferred the company of Lew and other local hunters. Since Tom never saw the need of replacing his worn out clothes, Lew would, every year or two, take him to the J.C. Penny store across the river in Atchison, Kansas for new overalls and shoes, always telling Tom that he had earned them. In more recent years I learned that Lew made sure that old Tom, when he died, had a decent burial. Few knew that Lew had also helped other poor souls in the community. It is a fact that this writer recalls accompanying him on a few such missions... all of which helps to enhance the moral status that was part of this man.

During those early years, Lew accepted a leadership role in his adopted home town of Rushville, serving on the village board and mayor from time to time. He had also begun to buy stock in the magazine, finally buying up all the shares from the two or three original owners. Now he was in charge of the entire operation. He therefore soon found that the printed product could best be produced by a large printing company in Kansas City, Missouri. They had vastly outgrown the home town print shop set up in the beginning. It was another good move on the part of the new owner, editor and publisher of The Red Ranger Magazine.

In retrospect it is revealing of Lew's instincts to consider how well known and respected he was among the "important" people in America during the first four or five decades of the twentieth century. He was on a first name basis with all the elected officials in Missouri as well as many big names residing in states such as Georgia, Mississippi, Texas, Kansas and Iowa. National political leaders must have recognized Lew's integrity and sought his support on numerous programs. One such person was Paul J. Rainey of Mississippi, then national leader of the Democrats. Mr. Rainey also owned substantial properties in Africa…and, he was a dedicated fox hunter. The two became fast friends bonding together on a number of conservation issues including the protection of the red fox *and* fox hounds. He was also believed to be one of the richest men in America, worth in the early nineteen twenties, eighty million dollars. Lew had received a long letter from Paul Rainey mailed from Boulogne, France suggesting they meet to discuss their first love, fox hunting, conservation and other matters. That was the last Lew heard from his friend as Paul died sailing for America on board a ship and was buried at sea.

A postscript to this story comes from Rainey's sister. She said that she wanted to establish a trust fund, amounting to $100,000 to fund a large fox hunt meet annually to honor her brother, Paul Rainey, who had no family of his own. Before Lew could respond she wrote to say that other leading hunters suggested the amount should be $500,000 and she wished for him to comment on this.

Lew thought such tactics were totally unwarranted and crass. He immediately answered, quietly saying that in his opinion it was terribly rude for "others" to request a larger sum for a gift and he would advise the sister, a Mrs. Rogers, to also withdraw the initial offer. So the lady did just that. For Lew Gingery there was never room to compromise on ethical issues.

One day early in his residence in Rushville, word reached

Lew of a secret meeting that evening at one of the lodge halls on main street. He was invited to attend. Early in the meeting he learned that some of the men in town were being asked to form a unit of the Ku Klux Klan. Though the story of what transpired is not a matter of physical record, I do recall hearing some of the details addressed. The extensive veranda of the Gingery home often attracted close friends and neighbors many years ago...whether Lew was home or not. From the audible whispers that evening I learned that Lew did attend the "recruitment" meeting. As soon as he was able to verify the organizing purpose of the gathering, he rose in anger and apparently delivered a blistering attack on the would- be leaders who were actually from out of town. In some well chosen words Lew sternly advised the local men to go back to their homes. Addressing the Klan recruiters, he rejected the concept as totally wrong and advised them bluntly to leave town and never return. That ended the meeting. No one ever knew who had invited the Klan people to come to the little community. In those years only one rather old bachelor Black man lived on a farm nearby. His name was John, whom everyone loved and who for awhile worked as a handy man in the area. Eventually he disappeared, moving elsewhere at the start of World War II. However, Lew's intervention at that organizing meeting was remembered long after the event took place.

In northwest Missouri, and more specifically, Buchanan County, the Democrat Party was dominant in those years. Candidates wishing to be successful would court Lew in Rushville asking for his support. Often his endorsement could help determine the outcome of a county race as well as some state wide contests in Missouri.

So it was no surprise to his friends when L.F. Gingery decided to respond to the ward leader in Saint Joseph who asked him to run for office. In 1930 he filed in the Democrat Primary for the Missouri State House of Representatives from Buchanan County. He won and also won handily in the general election that fall. During that two-year term, Lew more often than not opposed bills and programs that the "Tenth Ward Boss" in Saint Joseph recommended he support. He should have been aware of Lew's propensity for integrity while possessing a little bit of the rebel in his personae. So it was no real surprise that the "Boss", (a member of the Kansas City Pendergast Organization) brought forth another candidate to oppose Lew in the next Primary Election. Lew was defeated. However, he retained his sacred honor having again in that instance displayed reasons why this iconic individual will always be my favorite complete "Integer Man.

*   *   *   *

Author's Note

As readers will have surely acertained by now, Lewis F. Gingery was my father. I am the surviving youngest son.

In the year 1976, at his behest, my wife, Virginia and I brought Lewis back to Iowa. He had lost his devoted mate of more than sixty years, my gentle mother, Grace. And we had mourned the passing of his first son, a few years earlier. Almost all his friends and peers were gone. My sister and her family lived in California. So we found Lew a nice assisted lilving facility near us in Town. For a few months he literally "held court" dispensing wisdom and historical anecdotes, as he entertained large numbers of visitors who called on him. But after six months he became very tired; thus on the night of December 7, 1976 Lewis Francis Gingery, a uniquely compleete gentleman, our "Integer man" quietly died in his native Iowa. He was ninety seven.

INTEGER: Untouched, a compleete entity,whole, not fractional or mixed... from Websters Collegiate Dictionary

* * * *

REMOTE ARDNAMURCHAN
Sampling Scotland's Charm

It was the summer of 1987 when Virginia and I, natives of
middle America, booked a Saga Holidays Classical Europe
Tour that lasted about three weeks. Though we enjoyed visiting (and revisiting) some seven countries on the continent,
it was the new lasting friendships among several Europeans
made on that trip that are most memorable.

One couple, Jack and Joan Strevens, elicited a promise that
on a future holiday to the United Kingdom, that we pay them
a visit in Scotland. They live in a town named Kilmacolm
near Glasgow in the southwest of Scotland. Two years later
we made good on our vow and spent a week in the Strevens
home while exploring that historic section of the country.

A second invitation was extended to us two years later as
Jack had a special treat in mind for us, he said. He explained
that spring day, after we arrived and settled in, that he had
arranged with a friend to be our guide on a drive up into the
Highlands. Though we had rented in Maidstone that year a
surprising Avis upgrade, a handsome big Rover automobile,

Jack's friend volunteered to do the driving of his own car. Coincidentally, he had just acquired a new Rover, though smaller than our rental. But it proved to be large enough to accommodate all five of us.

Our man arrived on time right after breakfast on the appointed day. Jack did the introductions as we learned our guide's name. It was Bob Maule Bob is a congenial seasoned Scot, a veteran of travels in Scotland as he displayed a detailed map showing most of western Scotland. In that distinctive Scottish accent he explained that our goal was to drive north into the Highlands, often alongside various lochs and around mountains. Bob showed us on the map our destination. Pointing to a perceptible bulge of land, shaped a little like the head of a whale, far in the northwest, extending into the neighboring Sea of The Hebrides. It was quite a large area named Ardnamurchan. He then revealed that we would be visiting that *westernmost* part of Scotland and England, *that is not an island.* This became apparent to me when I traced the meridian north and south along the island- dotted western coastline of the UK. He explained that ours would be a two-day trip with an overnight in a tiny village only a few miles from the sea.

So we departed Kilmacolm on a typically overcast day for that part of the world, heading north up the 82 Road. Our guide, happily for us, recited a running account of the landmarks, various towns and bodies of water. It was an enjoyable learning experience for we two Americans. At one point Bob Maule referred to the little markers dividing the lanes as "cats eyes," as they reflected the car headlights at night.

Once, in traffic while ascending a hill behind a slowly moving car, Bob posed the question, "Shall we be twenty minutes late or twenty years early?"

Almost to himself, but audible to us, as he was on the lookout for a location said, "Tis bloody foolish tae forget the name of the town ye are lookin' for." Of course we did find it, as we threaded our way around hills and generally along the Firth of Lorn, and the extensive placid body of water named Loch Linnhe. As we approached another town which he named "Callendah" (Callendar) there was a sign that warned "15 MPH."

Bob's interpretation: "fifteen men peed here!"

Just beyond the city of Fort William, in the shadow of the highest mountain in the UK, Ben Nevis, we turned west and drove parallel to Loch Eil. As we climbed higher, the terrain became more wild. Signs of habitation became rare. But as we approached a curve in the road, there standing off to the side on an outcropping was a Scottish piper dressed in full regalia. Our Driver thoughtfully stopped the car allowing me to emerge with my 35 mm camera. The piper was alone and in that remote region, I have no idea how he was transported to that spot. He stood with dignity as I snapped off some film Then, I tossed a coin into an ordinary cap resting on the ground at his feet and with a wave of my hand, returned to the car. When we returned to America and to our home in Shenandoah, Iowa, we ordered that the several rolls of film from our trip be developed. When prints were returned to us, not one of the three or so shots I took of the kilted piper were to be found…nor was there evidence of the missing pictures on the negatives.

Since then I have read novels in which Celtic spirits have inhabited the Highlands of Scotland for centuries. Was I a witness of some esoteric, manifestation? In any event, the Piper was there, he was real…certainly no apparition.

About thirty minutes later we turned back south onto a

narrow but paved secondary road that led us past a gorgeous, naturalized collection of clear, mirror-like lochs well below us. On an opposite shore, there was an isolated cabin that was reflected perfectly on the mirror surface of that dark loch. Smoke rising from the chimney was also part of the image.

It was early in the afternoon when we arrived at the tiny village of Acharacle on Loch Shiel. Bob Maule explained that, "Ye have to sorta clear the throat when ye say the name o' this place." Acharacle gave evidence of no more than a dozen buildings. Bob had said that two houses served as bed and breakfast homes, so the Strevens claimed one and Virginia and I the other. A larger building we learned was the Acharacle Hotel where Bob would lodge that night. We would learn more of this building when we returned from the final jaunt that day out to the tip of Ardnamurchan After signing in at our chosen B&B, Bob collected us and we continued across the stark landscape to the very tip, the farthest point west (that is not an island) of the United Kingdom. Since leaving Acharacle we had not seen another human. A few sheep, of course, and a few brave sea birds were in evidence as living things. The coast was pebbled with rocks amid splashes of marsh grass stitched to miniature hillocks here and there. The tidal mud flats were dry and encrusted into approximate hexagons There was a narrow trail up a rather steep grade which led to the light house which was not staffed as it was operated remotely.

*Author, Lee and wife Virginia exploring the rugged
shoreline of Ardnamurchan, Scotland, Summer 1992*

So after absorbing the desolate seascape, part of the land "farthest west in Britain," we piled in the Rover and returned to our base, the village of Acharacle. Bob deposited us at our respective B& B and said he would pick us up for dinner. His passengers tried to guess how far we would have to drive to find a restaurant, for the prospects of finding one in that community seemed rather remote.

Never- the- less, our leader was at our door by the time he promised. That ride was less than five minutes duration as he parked near the door of the large building we knew to be a hotel. The weathered clapboard siding failed to generate much enthusiasm from his passengers, but with a smile on his face, Bob led us to the only door. We had entered a rather small pub with natural flora and fauna decorating the room, including an animal hide or two.

Bob obviously had been here before as he and the pair of Scot's behind the bar so indicated by their conversation. I do not recall what the others ordered. I only know that Bob suggested that I try his favorite single malt whisky, a premier brand from the Islay area off the coast. Laphroig. My sipping of two excellent Laphroig malts purchased by Bob Maule, may have affected my not recalling what the others ordered. In any event the appetizers were working for us all as we were famished. But, we thought, we must head out for that restaurant, right? Wrong. The lady bartender whispered to Bob who motioned conspiratorially for us to follow him through another door.

What met our eyes was totally unexpected. There before us was a fully appointed dining room including a glorious live fire place centered on one wall. We gazed at the chandeliers hanging from an ornate ceiling and to the luxuriou window treatments…, then our eyes rested on the table in the middle of the room. This table for five diners was set with the finest linen. Gleaming crystal and silver complimented each place setting of elegant bone China. And that was only the beginning. Our guide had learned earlier our entre preferences So that is what we were served, with appropriate courses before and after, including our first taste of an excellent pumpkin soup. Naturally, another aperitif and superb wines were also served. The incongruity of this setting in such a remote location made it seem like a fantasy and all the more appreciated. Most assuredly we gained an enhanced perspective of our new friend, Bob Maule.

The return drive back toward Fort William the following morning and subsequently to the Strevens home in Kilmacolm was quieter, as we were all trying to process our experiences. We did spend an hour or so in Fort William to do some souvenir shopping …later, some of us in the back seat dozed a little afterward as we retraced our route back to Jack and Joan's home.

Soon after we were unloaded, Jack said that Bob would be figuring up the apportioned cost of petrol, etc which we were delighted to share with our remarkable guide and driver. We soon said good by to Bob Maule and the next day, to the Strevens... and carried the memories of that exceptional experience in wonderful Scotland, which lives with us to this day.

* * * *

TOWN DRUNKS
An Essay of Remembrance

During the nineteen twenties and thirties most rural small towns in America included a *coterie* of drunkards. Rushville, Missouri was no exception. But first, so you aren't led astray, don't think for a minute that such an elitist term actually applied to individuals who lived in that era in mid-America. It's just that our little band of hard drinkers were totally unlike anyone else in that town of mostly hard working, morally righteous, no nonsense families. There was no bonding together either. They practiced alone, each with his own exclusiveness.

You have to think back in history to the days just before and immediately after prohibition. As a matter of fact, prohibition in our town didn't affect anyone much. The one saloon sold a beverage known as near beer before, during and after prohibition was repealed. Local governments simply said *no* to liquor. Only the bootleggers out in the county at some dark, semi-isolated spot who reaped the harvest of booze profits during those years in rural USA. Of course, the really important people in the illegal liquor pipeline were those with the capital and others daring to import certain spirits from Canada and abroad; pretty efficient, though outside the law

Now that we know the setting, let us talk about the four most memorable of those I am going to continue to define as Town Drunks. As a lad growing up through my early adolescent times, followed swiftly by those unremarkable teenage years, I have vivid recollections of these four colorful personalities.

Number one is Roundhead, Merritt

Physically, Roundhead was of medium height and very slender. When I first knew him he was probably in his late forties. His summer garb of overalls was always accented by a floppy, billed cap of indeterminate origin, resting on his head off center. Roundhead was not one of those embarrassing, falling- down type of drunkard, rather he was what I would call a staggerer when he was on his feet. Of course he spent many a day in the summer time sitting on the wooden front porch steps of Doc Sharpe's drug store in town. If he were ever employed at a job, no one told me and if there were work for him it wasn't steady. But he was good at conning folks out of a few coins when the spirit moved him...or as the need for spirits moved him. Which was often.

He lived up near the top of Doc Kane's Hill just a little way east of where we lived. He existed there with a brother Vern, who during those years was taken off now and then to spend a protracted time at the State's expense in the Big House (as they called it) in Jefferson City for some minor felony. If they had a mother or live- in wives during those years, I never saw them. But Vern had a wild son a bit younger than I who managed to stay out of serious trouble.

Whenever an election day approached, Roundhead would

become a predatory presence on main street. Since my dad was always involved in either running for the legislature or actively supporting a candidate, he was fair game for Roundhead prior to election day and especially *on* lection day. For example, dad's office dominated main street and if Roundhead caught a glimpse of his quarry exiting the doorway, he would pounce, if you could call wobbling up pouncing. He would squint his eyes and say something like, "Lew, fer a quarter I'll vote fer ya." Dad would usually try to ignore the initial pitch, but the guy would follow along as dad walked up the street to the post office. "All right, Lew, iffen you don't help me, I'll sure as hell vote *against* ye!" By now, any loafers leaning about were in a laughing fit and Dad was fit to be tied. More often than not Dad would give in and dig out a coin. Roundhead's unshaven face would break into a sly grin, showing his remaining yellow teeth and shuffle off. After all, two or three quarters would purchase a half pint or more of rotgut whiskey in those days. He found his smokes along the sidewalks where partially smoked cigarette butts would be tossed. Government safety nets, often called "Relief" for the poor and indigent, had not yet become law in America.

Though I don't think Roundhead Merritt ever really hurt anyone, but if he saw an item that had been laid carelessly about, it might be appropriated and, presumably, sold. After 1932, President Roosevelt's New Deal established the WPA to give men something to do to earn a bare living. Our Roundhead was not inclined to assume the appearance of gainful employment. How dare they even suggest such a thing! Panhandling didn't pay very much but he didn't have to do much more than suggest a little blackmail. Much more efficient.

By the time I returned from World War II, all the Merritts were gone from town, I know that Vern's son was in the military but didn't return to Rushville. I can speculate that Roundhead may have ended up in what we used to call the poor farm. None of those who live in Rushville today, know for sure, except that he is long gone.

Drunkard number two is Port "Hoot Owl" Conard.

Here is a character whose nickname seems to fit the first impression you got when you met him for the first time. His owl-like countenance was a family resemblance he shared with a brother and the brother's son. But it was Hoot Owl whose chief distinction locally was the fairly frequent bender in which he indulged. He is therefore included in this essay because of his obvious various degrees of public intoxication that were evident to me in those earlier decades of the twentieth century in our little town.

Not as colorful as Roundhead, Hoot Owl Conard was nevertheless dedicated in his apparent goal during his drinking bouts, of passing out in public. But The Owl was no mooch…he worked at odd jobs around the area. The first stages one recalls, involved his trudging up the little grade from his ramshackle house down by the creek, to reach our main street. All the while one could hear unintelligible muttering sounds uttered as he advanced.

Not the handsomest of men on his best days, when he was drunk, the Owl was downright homely. Even though beauty is in the eye of the beholder, when one beheld Hoot Owl, there was no contest. The clothes he pulled on every day were ordinary overalls and shirt that somehow always came close to matching his grizzled, bronzed, weathered countenance.

One of the more desperate events of the Owl's time in Rushville, that I can recall…which nearly everyone would term disgraceful, was when I found him passed out on the ground behind the barber shop. Though I can't recall how or why I came upon the scene, you should know the barber shop was directly across the street from Dad's office. In that open space adjacent to the walk leading to the entrance of the local Odd Fellows Lodge, I found Hoot Owl flat on his back, as if he were part of the refuse and trash normally found there. Around his neck one of the locals had placed an old discarded car tire. His head was resting on the tire and in his mouth someone had inserted a slightly used unlit cigar. I knew he was alive because I could see his cheeks alternately filling and expelling air on either side of the cigar. At the age of ten or eleven, I suppose it was a good temperance lesson for me early in my life. Obviously, his unconscious state eventually ended. One can speculate if he would ever guess how he assumed such an outlandish pose. But perhaps it never mattered to him.

Finally, as I said, Hoot Owl did work. Farm work in the area was his primary source of money and I know that his brother was usually gainfully employed as a tenant farmer in the countryside, and only occasionally went on a bender... and never as far as I can remember, became an exhibition down town. As with Roundhead Merritt, the Owl had removed from the area by the end of World War II. No one seems to know with certainty about any women in his life after his mother.

Town Drunkard number three is Bat Eye Yokum.

Here is a strange case of a middle- age man who would drink alcohol rarely but when he did become intoxicated his demeanor would change and he became *mean*. Kids my age knew that he had at one time been a boxer, though his skills never gained celebrity or even notoriety. But this part of his background sort of added to the aura, and potential danger of the guy.

Frankly, he makes this list mainly because of one early evening I found myself down town in Dalton Jones' Grocery Store when Bat Eye entered the store. It was immediately evident that he had been drinking heavily when I saw his eyes. They were bulging and bloodshot and they were looking straight at me. He mumbled something to another adult in the store and then began to amble toward me.

Now I was old enough to know that a drunkard is not *always* amusing nor someone you could laugh at with impunity. Alcohol works its effects in varying ways depending on the person involved. Believe me, that was my first lesson in that regard. I didn't have to read a book. Some times in life, first hand a priori experience is all one needs.

Anyway, when I could see that Bat Eye was heading for me I froze for a moment. I must have been not quite twelve because before I became a teenager, Dalton Jones sold out to Woody Tomlinson. (.Don't ask me why that store's ownership helps me fix the time in my mind, it just does.) Before I could take flight, Dalton stepped in front of me and persuaded Bat Eye to ease off. With that diversion, I made a beeline for the door and took off. At the time and forever after I have had no idea why I was the target of his apparent ire. Though I wasn't always the perfect little boy growing up in Rushville, I wasn't a pest either. Nor can I believe that he was angry with my father...I prefer to believe he mistook me for someone else, because after all, his vision had to have been impaired.

Bat Eye Yokum was smart, despite his penchant for booze. I believe in those years he helped his father -in-law in doing some light trucking in the area. He was a stocky, well built man of perhaps 5 feet eight inches in height. He was always dressed fairly neatly. His wife, Dolly, was a tiny thing, not unattractive and very pleasant. We kids absorbed the gossip that Dolly ruled the roost of that very small house on main street just east of the lumber company/hardware store. We guessed that booze may have been an outlet for Bat Eye's occasional bender.

Over the years since that incident, I know Bat Eye was semi reformed. When my dad sold his business in the nineteen fifties, it was Bat Eye who bought that building on main street. By then he had actually lost his nickname and was known as Mr. Norman Yokum. He opened a fairly good sized antique operation in the building. For the record, my mom was one of his better customers for a few years. Eventually he gave up the business and, as far as I know, he became a recluse until he died.

Town Drunkard number four is Vern Donaldson.

It somehow bothers me to think of Vern Donaldson as a "town drunk". Yes, I remember late evenings in the summer time when he would be quite drunk but he was so very kind to everyone. And he was one of the strongest, hardest workers, anyone ever saw.

During those summer evenings in our home town, kids like me would gravitate to the main street under one of the two street lights and devise games of dare- base, king's- base and so on. If we were lucky, Vern Donaldson, huge, Paul Bunyonesque Vern, would seat himself on a curb by the bank building and stare at the gutter. He must have been almost six and a half feet tall and weighed...who knows? A lot. Usually some brazen kid would challenge him to see how many of us he could lift over his head from a sitting position. Amazingly, he would heft two or three of us sixty pound or so, boys and hold us like that for a few seconds. All in good humor. And none of us felt, I am certain, to comment or make fun of his over indulgence. After thirty or forty minutes of that kind of display, Vern would tire of the sport and walk off into the dark toward his house down by the railroad tracks. As you must suspect, we kids really liked him and obviously he put up with us.

By the time I was a senior in high school I had personally witnessed Vern Donaldson's prowess at work in at least two areas. My dad always knew if he had a job that required enormous strength he would call on Vern. For example, there was the year he dug a cistern beside one of the barns on the forty acre farm on the edge of Rushville. He kept two men busy hauling up large buckets of that loess-like soil for no more than three days until he had reached a depth of twenty five or thirty feet. He never complained or moaned about anything. Vern just worked! The two or three days I joined him on the farm pitching hay is still memorable. After the tenant farmer would deliver our full rack of hay to the barn, Vern always climbed up into that stifling hot loft and almost effortlessly spread around the hay that was lifted and deposited by the built-in giant fork. I know from the rare instances I had that job it was cruelly unpleasant. But Vern Donaldson seemed to thrive on hard work.

Now you know why I am reluctant to paint Vern with the same brush as the others. If he were a drunkerd he was the most cooperative, benign, hard drinker in my life-long recollection.

When I returned to Rushville after World War II, I learned that following what must have been an exceptionally bad day for him, Vern got drunk and hanged himself from a tree in the front yard of his house. His survivors included five or six tow-headed children and a wife. They left town shortly after my favorite giant ended his sad life. It is sad because I doubt if anyone in Vern's life ever told him, in some respects, he was magnificent, or at the very least, worthwhile.

* * * *

WINNEBAGO FROM HELL

Have you ever dreamed of a fun idea, worked it all out in your mind, sold it to everyone and then have that wonderful experience shattered by forces, (mostly) beyond your control?

Read on and hear my story.

The month of March in 1970 was when it all started. The Gingery family of Shenandoah, Iowa, all five of us, would rent a very large motor home, drive it to a friend's house south of Houston Texas, sightseeing on the way and camping whenever and wherever we felt like it. And on and on. Perhaps you know the drill.

First we needed to find the vehicle. No problem. A classified ad in the Omaha World Herald described one such motor home, a Winnebago, large enough to accommodate the five of us. I called the number given and at the appointed time late in the afternoon, after my day at the office, all five of us drove to the parking lot on south Thirteenth St. and saw it sitting there with the owner nearby. Of course the RV had the mandatory toilet and a tiny cell- like shower stall… A mini fridge, tiny kitchen, etc. Everything *looked* to be in order.

After a brief consultation, my wife Ginnie and I chose to close the rental deal. After shaking hands with the owner and exchanging copies of the rental agreement, it was time to take the Winnebago home to Shenandoah. Not quite twelve-year-old son Scott chose to ride with me in the big coach, which I immediately learned was no touring car. Ginnie, soon to be sixteen-year-old Lynn and Laura who was almost five followed us in the family Olds.

Though it was already dark I had no trouble negotiating the exit to Thirteenth St. and headed up the hill toward the south Omaha bridge over the Missouri River. As we motored along near the top of the hill the engine sputtered and began to cough. And *I* began to sweat, looking frantically for the gas gauge. Yep the needle was on the red. But then a rare piece of luck happened. I spotted a gas station on the right side of the street. As we pulled to the pumps the engine literally stopped dead. Of course Scott was curious as to why we had to stop so soon. Fortunately, he never heard my response. Ginnie drove up behind and wondered also until she saw the chagrin so obvious on my face. So, we just screwed up by assuming the tanks were full! I repeat "tanks" as both, including the reserve were empty. Some will recall that in those days gas prices hovered around a half dollar a gallon. Anyway, the gas flowed from the hose seemingly forever. At that time, twenty dollars for gas was a fortune. And I hadn't yet realized that the milage per gallon for this Winnebago might average ten miles to the gallon with a *tail* wind. Against the wind, much less.

Well, undeterred by this first surprise, Scott and I led our two-vehicle caravan across that ancient bridge and on to Shenandoah some sixty miles away. We refused to believe a minor glitch like empty gas tanks could spoil this special holiday. Rather than block our garage driveway I maneuvered the motor home onto the adjoining side street, Seventh Avenue. You may assume correctly that the monster drew some attention from our friends and neighbors the next day as we began to load it with provisions, some individual clothes and bed clothes. All five of us made numerous trips inside the coach and out during the process of loading the next day.

As we were nearing the departure time early in the afternoon that day, I noticed some commotion at the door of the unit. Her two older siblings were coaxing Laura, who was inside the unit, to unlock the door that she had locked accidently or it had secured itself closed without help. She failed to find the switch so she was in tears and her brother and sister were totally exasperated. Finally, I managed from the outside to pry open one of the small side windows at the front passenger side. We forced it wide enough to accommodate Scott whom I boosted into the opening. So he unlocked the door and rescued his little sister. Portent of things to come? No, just a tiny crisis, averted.

By mid afternoon we waved goodby to the neighbors and began our odyssey. We were all in high spirits as we headed into the lowering sun. Our route, laid out in advance would take us southwest out of our corner of Iowa through a part of Nebraska into northeast Kansas. After about seventy five miles I was adjusting to the size and driving eccentricities of that huge motor home. The built-in radio even had a tape player accompanied by a single Dean Martin tape which I began to enjoy in an almost relaxed posture.

My reverie was intruded upon by the sudden, familiar sense that a tire was going flat. We pulled over, stopped and all the bodies sifted out of the coach to visually verify the problem. Yes indeed, a rear tire was flat. Of course my first question was, do we have a spare tire? or did the owner stiff us on that item also. Not to worry. Nicely affixed directly under the rear of the unit was the spare tire in its rack. And it really did have air in it.

So there, while it was almost dark, on a seldom used road in Kansas with all family members helping, we jacked up the unit and changed tires. After quickly putting the bad tire back into the bracket we drove off in search of a place to park for the night. I found a place fairly close to a gasoline station (always a prudent thing to do, I learned.) Mother Ginnie and Lynn cleverly prepared a nice meal before we chose to retire for the night. So far, so good right? Wrong. There was no nearby electrical hook-up so we turned on the generator to produce some heat as early March in our latitude is a bit brisk, especially at night. Now, one would think that the thermostat would determine the performance of the heater/generator. Not for us. I spent a good part of that night turning off and on the generator which produced exceedingly high tempera-tures when the noisy thing was running.

Finally, morning came. We opened up the curtains and found the weather, at least, was most favorable. After each of us taking a turn in the midget toilet/bathroom, we had breakfast. Afterward, we again filled up the tank with gas at the nearby station then turned the correct blunt end of the Winnebago toward Oklahoma.

At some point during that day Scott who was in the very back of the coach shouted to me,

"Dad, we just lost a tire. It's rolling back the way we came." Now, years after that event, I find it incredible that the flat-tened tire and wheel actually rolled perhaps a hundred yards up to the very door of a filling station. So we drove back to retrieve it and with help, put it back into its bracket more securely this time. I thanked the station attendant and we drove off. Yes, I said we drove off without getting the flat fixed at that place. As I mentally berated myself for being so stupid, I found there in Oklahoma soon, another station where we did get the flat repaired, plus another large measure of gasoline.

By the third day we were grooved in to motoring and living in the Winnebago environment. You don't suffer the nights gladly, however. Parking the rig in a semi-lighted area as we always tried to do meant traffic and noise... even in that rare rest center. The advantage of choosing rest centers when they are available. is the accompanying customary toilet and lavatory facilities. After a few days of using the unit's "bath room" most of us would be on the lookout for a place where body necessities might be performed where one did not have to be a contortionist. Moreover, you have to realize that dumping the toilet holding tank was a major operation. First we had to find a suitable RV Park or its reasonable equivalent. Also, I would have to unlock and unleash the hose from the compartment under the unit, and so on. Therefore, I must admit at this late date that the refuse holding tank was never emptied. God only knows when it had been drained before we took possession of the Winnebago.

After a few days along the way it was evident that one did not flush the stool while we were moving along the roads and highways. There was a back draft that sent an odor, if not noxious, it was thoroughly unpleasant throughout the van when this happened. Did the factory designers or workers add that feature as a private joke or was it just one more defect in our unit? In any event we all got the word, no one uses (or flushes) the potty while we are in transit. But one day as we were well into Texas, Scott forgot and did flush the stool.

I immediately caught the odor up front in the "pilots seat." Glancing in the rear view mirror I glimpsed Scott emerging from the bathroom literally trying to "swim out" to escape the invisible methane cloud. Of course only Scott failed to see the humor of that situation.

Our initial destination, as has been said earlier, was the Houston, Texas area. More precisely, we planned to meet my former World War II crewmate's family who resided in the small town of Pearland. Our waist gunner, Dr. Lloyd Ferguson, was the superintendent of the large school system that serves the NASA community and we hadn't seen each other for twenty five years. Also, living nearby was another member of our crew, Kenny, our navigator, whose life since the war had been less than successful. But we chose to call on him and his wife and two children who invited us in and insisted we spend the night in their house. Unfortunately, the older child, a boy in his mid twenties was mentally challenged from birth. A teenage daughter showed signs of an assumed maturity beyond her years. Ginnie, Laura and I were assigned the boy's room. It was virtually bare of furniture which was okay. But the floor of the only closet was covered with dolls whose eyes were indelicately poked out! Lynn and Scott wisely chose to overnight again in the Winnebago. Laura, Ginnie and I huddled together in the one bed. Very early the next morning we bid our hosts adieu and made for the motor home to continue the short drive to the Fergusons.

As we suspected, Lloyd, Rosalie and their two sons rolled out the red carpet for us. Needless to say, the accommodations were very comfortable. It was a delightful visit which included an evening in a restaurant high above Houston where we were joined by Kenny and his wife. Later we celebrated Easter with our friends as Lynn observed her sixteenth birthday on this visit.

* * * *

Finally it was time to say goodby. Retracing our route we reached the northern outskirts of Houston when we heard a bang!…bump, bump, bump. When we pulled into a nearby Texaco station it was very clear that one of our tires suffered a blow-out. This was another down side to record. The slim up side was that the Texaco station also boasted a mechanic.

After a cursory assessment of the problem, we were directed toward the edge of the property, near a drainage ditch partially filled with water. Since it was obvious we were not continuing our trip home immediately, the youngsters began to explore the ditch. It took all of their mother's powers of persuasion to keep them corralled. After all, it was an unknown area to us and traffic on the nearby thoroughfare was at times intense.

Finally after at least an hour the mechanic took the wheel off and declared that the blow-out was caused by overheated brake bands. His prognosis:

"Yep, I can repair it, but you'al better fix to stay put for a while since I got to order new parts from Houston."

"How long will that take?"

"I ought to have 'em by near this time tomorrow." Having no better options, I suggested he proceed with as much speed as he could muster.

*Scott and Laura (with differing points of view) at
north edge of Houston, Texas...awaiting repair
of brakes and new tire for the Big UNIT.*

Since the van was resting on a mechanic's jack in the rear,
we could continue to live inside, which was good (nothing
better nearby) Budget? HA HA Anyway, the van was secure
and we did have beds inside.

Suffice it to say that Ginnie's ingenuity was taxed to the
utmost to find creative endeavors for our three lively children.
By all means, the drainage ditch became off limits which of-
fended son Scott just a little. Also, the ground on the station
side of the vehicle was mostly tar, oil and gravel. Not a very
pretty playground. As I recall, there were lots of old standby
playing card games and probably some new ones invented
during that more than thirty hour period of time.

It is perhaps redundant to report that I retained a record of
the mechanic's invoice for the labor and parts required. Finally
we were ready to re engage the highway back to Shenandoah.
The owner of the Winnebago back in Omaha would therefore

be advised of the charges when we returned the vehicle to him. By now, our moods were definitely not spiritual toward that person. Would we seek recompense? In the words of that other Iowan, John "Duke" Wayne, "You'd better believe it, Pilgrim."

However, first we had several hundred miles to travel. Naturally, Ginnie and I were asking ourselves, What more can happen? Two days later, on April 1st, April Fools Day, near the town of Horton, Kansas we found out. We ran smack into a spring snow storm on a highway without any visible places to pull out or exit. As you may assume, driving that boxy shaped motor home in a high wind is a little like carrying a large pane of glass or plywood across the street in a hurricane. Of course, the visibility was almost nil. Having driven our own cars many times to Colorado on ski trips we often encountered snow. But herding a Winnebago in a High Plains blizzard will test one's driving skills never before realized.

Finally, after at least an hour of unmitigated tension, we were able to see a turn off …yes, fortunately near a filling station. And it was there we spent the night. Though it took a little while for my hands to uncurl completely from the steering wheel grasp, we all had a warm drink and relaxed while the swirling wind and snow continued to pelt us. But we stayed put. Though it was unreasonable and quite wrong to blame the motor home owner for the blizzard, I managed to do so.

The next morning we found the sky was blue, the winds subsided and we could see traffic moving on the highway. After a bite to eat and another refill of gasoline, we wrestled the unit out onto the highway once more.

By around noon that day, April 2nd, we arrived home at our wonderful big white house on Elm Street in Shenandoah.

There was little snow left on the ground and so the kids all exploded from the unit to give their own reports to their friends. For Ginnie and for me we made silent vows, "never again," and began making a list of items and thoughts we would deliver the next day to Mr. RV owner in Omaha... along with the Winnebago...the Winnebago from Hell.

Later that month following the terminus of this adventure, three other couples, close friends, convened at our house for our monthly Dinner/Bridge occasion. Of course, we were prompted to describe our trip to the Houston, Texas area, which resulted in much amusement by our friends. It was suggested that I "write up" this story. I just did.

PS: The owner of the Winnebago did comply, giving us full credit for the repairs.

* * * *

OH TEACHER!

The Rushville, Missouri Public School year, in 1939, began again early in September. I was in the senior class and still only sixteen years old. For the first time in the existence of the school system in our small town, the School Board hired an instructor of "Commerce." At least that was the term used to describe two new courses to be taught that year. We Junior and Senior students only knew that typing and shorthand would now be offered…as electives, I believe. The teacher would represent a new face among the faculty. Her name: Miss Mary Kay Lichty.

As background, one must know that the new school building, completed the previous year, housed classrooms that accommodated grades one through twelve. Elementary and high school grades were separated by an excellent gym where boys basketball and girls volleyball would practice and compete. (In prior years the teams played in the IOOF Lodge hall above Roy Bunten's garage down town.) The new school provided a separately partitioned area on the high school side of the gym in which the commerce courses would be taught.

A total of seven teachers were employed in those days, three would preside on the elementary side, Four teachers handled the students from grades nine through twelve on the opposite side. A man was hired as Superintendent and another man was hired signed to handle the coaching of athletics. I don't recall if the coach also taught. Doubtless I would have known since he would surely have been as ineffective in the class room as he was at coaching. It was apparent that he knew very little about competitive sports, so most of the coaching of basketball and baseball my senior year was in the capable hands of our best athlete, Tink Cooper.

It was a time when women readily found employment in the profession of teaching...usually when other less specialized jobs were not available. Whether coincidentally or not, most of our women teachers were unmarried, a few barely out of their teens. Rarely did any of those women, young or not so young, rate more than a passing glance in the halls of our Rushville School. Since many of the teachers in our small town rented rooms in established homes, we seldom if ever met them on main street, in the few shops or in church. At least that is my recollection.

Enter our new Commerce teacher:

So I confess that when we young, energetic lads in high school caught the first glimpse of Miss Mary Kay Lichty, several of us rushed with barely disguised alacrity to sign up for typing that first semester. For you see, Miss Lichty was more than merely pretty, she was in our eyes, *glamorous*. But mainly she was young (probably no more than twenty one or twenty two.) Her skin and features were, in our minds, flawless. She was tall and slim and in her high heels, cast a most delightfully classy aura as she demonstrated the correct system of touch typing. When Miss Lichty moved close to a student at the typewriter making sure our clumsy fingers were placed correctly on the keyboard, her scent was …my goodness, nice. If testosterone could have been measured in that classroom in those days there is no doubt we guys would have rocketed it off the chart at the beginning of that course.

Having done well in typing that semester, I chose to take shorthand the last semester of my senior year, partly because of Miss Lichty, but mostly out of curiosity. Actually, I rather enjoyed the experience of learning that mysteriously flowing Gregg system. . . Quite soon, however, upon graduation, I found that shorthand skill became for the most part, perishable as far as I was concerned. But it was the course in typing that stayed with me, with practice, and was one of my better decisions as a young person in that school system.

After my service in the military in World War II, in college and in business, the knowledge and use of the standard typewriter keyboard has been essential to one who chose journalism, advertising and marketing as a profession.

So that is one reason why I am so glad that pretty Mary Kay Lichty came to our school system in Rushville, Missouri that day in the year 1939. I have no recollection of her tenure there. I only know she was one of those excellent teachers whose influence was an enduring part of my public school experience.

Sweeping away the mists of time, I say today in the twenty first century, "Thank you Mary Kay Lichty."

Lee Emerson Gingery

* * * *

CHOO-CHOO TRAINS

This descriptive name was widely used by parents and kids early in the Twentieth Century identifying those picturesque trains cris-crossing the entire United States. The very sound made by the enormous engine belching smoke and hissing steam made the Choo-Choo expression fit the scene. Early in America's Swing Music era, circa 1940, the hugely popular Glen Miller Band performed and recorded the memorable *Chattanooga Choo Choo* number. Even now in the twenty first century one may hear daily, certainly in that Tennessee city, the catchy lyrics and bouncy instrumental phrasing of the song.

It was not until the nineteen thirties when these steam engine powered behemoths, fueled by coal, were *beginning* to be supplanted by the elegant streamlined engines propelled by fuel described in a later time as electromatic diesel.

But this is not about the history of those continent shrinking monsters. Rather this essay will discuss train rides this writer recalls beginning with that short trip from Saint Joseph, Missouri en route to the Fort Leavenworth, Kansas military reception center. There I became a recruit in the U.S. Army early in 1943 during World War II.

Before that event, I was able to see and marvel at the trains chugging north and south past the edge of our little town, Rushville, Missouri. Also, I heard my father describe his business trips on trains. He always recalled how well he would sleep in one of those early Pullman Sleeping Cars. Dad felt he was lulled by the universally described "clickity clack" sonorescence of iron wheels on the iron tracks. (Now many rails are made much longer and welded end to end I understand, with iron wheels emitting a sound more like a "whoosh" along the landscape.)

After initial processing at Fort Leavenworth, Kansas just days later, a large number of us, newly sworn-in army privates, stepped into several rail cars attached to one of those magnificent steam engines revealing to us the very essence of the World War II troop train. It was early spring and that year quite warm. So before marching out to board the train we were advised to don our summer uniforms called euphemistically, "sun tans." The balance of our new wardrobes was stuffed into barracks bags and tossed into a baggage car, I assume. We did manage to keep our shaving kits and tooth brushes close at hand.

For five days we newly minted GIs were treated to our first look at the American South and West. It became much warmer during each succeeding day that year so that the windows were opened allowing free access for the smoke and soot coming from the engine smoke stack to permeate the rail cars. Within three days our uniforms were sweaty and dark from the hot, smoky environment arrangements. There was a dining car providing basic boxed lunches two or three times a day. In the back of our car was a cubby hole rest room containing a tiny metal lavatory and a stool that was a grown-up cousin of the ubiquitous convenience or "slop jar" found in many homes in that era. In cubic feet the latrine spaces were even smaller than present- day air liner toilets of this more modern age. Imagine fifty or so of us in each rail car queuing up awaiting one's turn to perform necessary ablutions. Flushing and lavatory drainage were deposited on the rail bed below. So much for hygiene and environmental purity.

Sleeping accommodations were practically nil as there were no Pullman-like bunks in any of *our* rail cars. Therefore throughout the five days on that train, if we slept it was in one of the seats…probably next to a buddy. Since we all smelled of the same sweat and grime, no one complained as none of us had any authority. The person in charge was a corporal who undoubtedly was also a private, until recently.

After passing through semi-arid sections of the states of Texas with bits of New Mexico and Arizona thrown in, often shunted on sidings or halted, I was aware early on the fourth day that our train had once again stopped. I looked out an open window to survey my first view of a desert landscape. Later I learned t hat we had paused, probably to add water or coal at the town of Needles, California. Beyond a scattering of buildings I took in the arid desolation of sand and various species of cactus in the Mojave desert For a lad of the mostly green Great Plains, the view was mesmerizing.

So the continuation of that train ride, finally on the fifth day brought us to our destination, the art- deco train station in Las Angeles, California. We gratefully left that train, a bedraggled pathetic lot, I am sure, only to quickly board a number of military buses. Heading south, the convoy carried us until almost midnight, finally halting at a coastal Army basic training base we learned was named Camp Callan. The buses deposited us near the headquarters of C Company, of 55th Battalion. This episode of my Train Experience ended ig-nominiously since mine was the only barracks bag that failed to make the scene. So the next morning and for several days I was forced to wear my dirty, stinking sun tans that first week while learning to march in close order and memorizing the important manual of arms, etc. Within six days, Glory Be, I was issued new clothes.

My sought after transfer several weeks later to the Army Air Corps Flying Cadets did not involve, at first, a train ride. This time I took an ordinary bus to Santa Ana Army Air Base in Southern California. But having passed all the IQ screening tests at Santa Ana, I was ordered to ship out from Camp Callan a few days later and was subsequently assigned to the Cadet orientation station in Amarillo, Texas. This time I would *not* travel via a troop train, per se. My travel docu-ments called for me to ride the train much as a civilian, but in my Class A uniform. What a delight! Actually no more than a long day and a half travel time ensued that October depositing me finally at Amarillo.

By early the following year the more than a hundred of our contingent of new cadets learned that all the training schools were filled. Since the war effort needed more "boots on the ground," than Air Corps pilots and crewmen…High Com-mand therefore, saw us as an untapped pool from which to draw. As a result nearly all my cadet classmates were sent di-rectly to Europe to fight the war as infantrymen. Young men were also being taken from other Army Specialized Training Schools for the same reasons. By the luck of the draw, how-ever, I was assigned to an Army Air Force radio school at Sioux Falls Army Air Base in South Dakota. I recall that the trains transporting me to Sioux Falls were quite ancient. In fact, one car on that last leg of the trip was heated by a small, primitive coal burning stove. There is nothing in my notes nor my memory of the rail line or lines we used to reach my destination. I do recall that it was quite cold when I arrived at that Air Force radio school at Sioux Falls.

After graduation six months later my class was sent to Yuma, Arizona to train as radio operator gunners. This assignment was routine in the parlance of the day. Our numbers this time were smaller so that I had my first experience in Pullman Car accommodations. It was on that train ride that I recalled my father's admonition to guard against the ever-present thievery that might occur aboard sleeping cars. So I inserted my billfold containing no more than about ten dollars inside my pillow case. Awaking the next morning at the Air Force Gunnery station at Yuma I hurriedly dressed and disembarked the train with my fellow radio school graduates looking for base transportation. Just as the Yuma bus appeared, I realized that my billfold was not in its usual place in a hip pocket. The train pulled away before I could reboard it to retrieve my personal property from its hiding place inside that pillow case. I never saw it again but the Pullman porter undoubtedly was pleased to find in my bunk a ten dollar gratuity for his services.

After the six week late summer training cycle in that suffocating desert environment our class graduated with radio operator-gunner's wings and the stripes of corporals. We were now fully qualified for air combat in one of the Air Corps bomber aircraft. Thus our contingent once again boarded a troop train that transported us back east with a stop to change trains at the busy Kansas City Union Station. There was barely enough time allowed to seek and climb aboard another designated north-bound troop carrier. Again, our train was pulled by one of those wonderful steam engines as we swiftly rocked along the old Burlington rails north past my home town, Rushville, Missouri. Our destination was Lincoln, Nebraska Army Air Field. Here, my fellow grads of the Yuma school would be outfitted with flying suits, oxygen masks, throat microphones, heavy boots and flight jackets plus (for officers and radio operators) the uniquely important G I wrist watch, preparatory to joining our assigned crews whom we would meet at the next base.

That training base, officially named a Replacement Training Unit, was in the vicinity of Dyersburg, Tennessee. Which of course ordained that we would travel on a fast moving train south all the way to Dyersburg Army Air Field. The morning after our arrival my radio men comrades and I were able to meet the other members of our assigned nine man crew. New, close relationships soon evolved as we performed our specialties training in the large Boeing B-17 Flying Fortress aircraft.

Roughly six weeks later, my excellent crew of nine members completed the intensive day and night practice missions in the skies above Tennessee, Arkansas and Southeast Missouri, with an occasional cross country flight tossed in. After completing our training, once more we boarded a troop train, and again headed for Lincoln, Nebraska.

The speed of our trains began to increase now with every succeeding advancement of our training skills…moving us closer to actual combat. So this stay in Lincoln was abbreviated, somewhat. We tossed away the bulky boots, pants and jackets supplied earlier for the latest flight jackets and other necessary accouterments such as holstered hand guns, heated flying pants and boots. Newly outfitted and carrying promotions in rank, we again boarded another train bound for the

Northeastern United States. We were informed that we were headed for a port of embarkation in New Jersey.

This train moved with surprising velocity, rarely stopping and it seemed, hardly slowing. On this trip we were supplied by the familiar boxed lunch prepared by the famous roadside entrepreneur, the Fred Harvey Restaurants. The American military of those days usually found a touch of humor in almost every activity. It was said, for example, that the last spoken words by that Harvey was: "Slice that ham thin,boys, slice that ham thin."

So this last troop carrier for me was that non-stop ride to Camp Kilmer in New Jersey where we were swept aboard the massive British Ocean liner Queen Elizabeth. Five and a half days later we docked in Greenock, Scotland. Welcome to the United Kingdom!

Post Scripted observation to Trains: During my time in Great Britain during the war there were several occasions when I, as an American Serviceman, would ride trains in that Island nation. But first, after disembarking, from the ship we were directed to a train backed into position for our boarding. Immediately, apple-cheeked, attractive young Scottish "lassies" of the "King's Army" passed down the isles dispensing tea and shortbread treats. We all agreed: "Now this is how one should fight a war."

Finally, the configuration of the British passenger cars was unique to me. Seats were arranged so that three people might sit opposite, facing three others. Also, some compartments opened directly to the station platforms. But the sound of the train whistles, was quite different, …emitting a very high- pitched blast when approaching intersections. Since those days we have all seen and heard these British train sounds in many romantic motion pictures filmed on location in England through the years. All these experiences reside in my memory of long ago as part of the lore of "Choo Choo Trains.

* * * *

Late in the 20th Century, the old reliable passenger train lines found themselves in financial trouble. Passenger traffic was fading...The new Interstate Highway system made traveling by automobile a reliable mode of travel. So the federal government proceeded to take over the passenger lines. The familiar names such as Santa Fe and Burlington, among others were replaced by a system named Amtrak...subsidized and managed by the government. Many of us early in the twenty first century know that is a recipe for failure! Following is a recent Amtrack Experience.

Since our son, a retired U.S Navy officer and his family, live in the state of Virginia, my wife and I have either flown commercial or driven our autos from our home in Southwest Iowa to York County in Virginia...never finding these options completely satisfying. So we all thought, "Why not try Amtrak? Therefore, some four months before we would be departing from the town of Creston, Iowa eighty miles away, I purchased tickets covering the round trip for which I paid almost twelve hundred dollars.

On the day before our scheduled trip, July 31, 2009, we drove to Creston where we lodged in a motel for that night (since the east bound "California Zephyr" was scheduled to arrive at 8:04 am on August 1.) No problems so far as the next morning we loaded our car with our three bags after checking out of the motel and were at the *unmanned station* well before the advertised arrival time of Train # 6 destined for Chicago. That train arrived two hours late. So we made it on board finding our reserved seats. Arrival in Chicago was chaos. There was very little time to catch the Capitol Limited to Washington DC on which we had reserved a "sleeping room." Since time was short for boarding, a host of red caps began gathering passengers and baggage transporting us to our trains, right there in the lower track area. It was a bit hazardous but no real problems. Sleeping that night, however, proved elusive as Virginia and I are no longer contorted and flexible enough to fit in those upper and lower bunks on which there was no head room for us, two normal sized, senior adults. Thus we spent the daylight hours seated in the lounge car from which we could see the passing scene of the lush, green states of Iowa, Illinois, Indiana and points east and north.

I can recall with nostalgia the lovely dining cars on various train trips we had taken years earlier. No longer does that impression exist on the trains we experienced this time. The menu that we tested with trepidation was universally bad. The persons in charge, usually surly. But the most unsatisfactory aspect of the trip, going and coming, was that our trains ran late, very late. Another annoying problem happened on the last leg on our homeward bound segment. We were assigned seats in a nicer car that soon filled with families of children of all ages whose parents headed directly for the lounge car leaving their kids unsupervised to roam about and actually run and skip from one end of the moving car to the other. And the tracks were, on that stretch, universally rough…My wife and I sat in our position even reluctant to get up to visit the filthy toilets.

However, all this being said I must admit that spending several days with our son and his family in his home on the shore of the Chesapeake Bay was delightful, despite the horrendous traveling conditions on Amtrack.

* * * *

Buzzing Helgoland With
The Brass ...In A B-17

The following incident took place near the end of the war, or possibly soon after the war in Europe was concluded. Frankly there is nothing in my wartime diary that mentions it or the timeing. I did mention this mission briefly in our 351st Bomb Group periodical published a few years ago, but not with the details included here. Anyway, I can still recall vividly in my mind that flight to Helgoland.

As air crew veterans of our 351st Bomb Group base at Polebrook in East Anglia, England will recall, every time a B-17 leaves the ground and soars aloft it must have on board, besides the obvious two pilots, three additional crewmen. These would be a navigator, flight engineer and a radio operator. I have no recollection of the criteria used to select the three additional crewmen for this flight, I only know on that very day I was named to fill the familiar seat of radio operator. Certainly I was told that we planned to fly to the island of Helgoland...so I probably volunteered! Therefore, as I took my position in the radio room the pilot, a lieutenant colonel and the co-pilot, a major climbed aboard. Earlier, a navigator and flight engineer joined me as my crew mates.

So where is Helgoland? (*Heligoland*, in the original Frisian, I think.) Actually it is a tiny island, really an archipelago in the North Sea, about two hours by sea from the mouth of the River Elbe. For several hundred years, even before the Napoleonic wars, Helgoland was critical to the nation holding the island. Ownership was claimed at one time separately by Denmark, Britain and Germany. It was held by Germany during World War II and became an important base for the German submarine fleet. And therein tells the tale of why we chose to visit Helgoland on that beautiful day in the spring of 1945.

There was no altimeter in those B-17 Flying Fortress radio rooms. So I can only guess that we must have flown well below 8,000 feet en route north from Polebrook. Upon reaching Helgoland I can recall circling the main island. After locating the coastal area that held the once fearsome, and heavily defended submarine pens we zoomed toward the sea. Through my window I could see clearly the various openings at sea level into the wall of that little island. I can vouch chafe we were, it seemed to me, inches from the surface of the North Sea. But after each dive, the pilot would in a timely manner pull back the control column and climb to gain more momentum for the next pass.

Soon it became apparent there was a quasi legitimate reason for this venture. The major had a camera and recorded the sub pen openings from several different vantage points from our B-17. I will admit that at one point I also unfastened my safety belt and got a brief terrific view of our "target" from the waist gunner's position. I have no recollection of the number of passes we made. Suffice it to say that views of the damaged Nazi sub pens were well recorded on film.

I never knew the names of the pilots. At the end of operations at Polebrook we counted a goodly number of field grade officers. I would have recognized Major Mort Korges, our 509th CO, so it was not he with the camera. Nor do I recall the names or rank of the navigator or flight engineer. I asked myself if perhaps the lieutenant colonel or major had visited Helgoland on a mission during the war. However, the only evidence I could find in our book of missions is one passing reference to a crew encountering some flak coming from the "Frisian Islands." Having recalled this event to our son, (a retired Navy commander) Scott suggested that considering the strategic importance of Helgoland, and the emergence of the Soviets, this *may have been* part of an Intelligence survey. Who knows?

After sixty plus years, I suppose it is remarkable that I can even *recall* that strange "Buzzing Helgoland" flight. But trust me, it happened!

* * * *

A JOURNEY TO REMEMBER

N ow, in 21ˢᵗ Century America, some sixty five years after
the end of World War II, we find stories and pictures
of groups of British and French citizens more fully cogni-
zant of the dominant roles we Americans played in that war.
Therefore, I am reminded of the events that took place when
surviving members of my 8ᵗʰ Air Force, Flying Fortress, 351ˢᵗ
Bomb Group met in reunion at our old air base just outside
the hamlet of Polebrook, East Anglia, England. Following are
recollections of that reunion that took place in June of the
year 2000… jointly remembered by Lee and Virginia Gingery
of Shenandoah, Iowa.

As our flight and all the others originating in the USA
landed at Airports in London we were met by busses ordered
by David Gower. David, but a child during the war, has been
our loyal advocate and reliable host at Polebrook Airfield. He
began this volunteer duty just a few years after we Americans
departed the United Kingdom in June, 1945. So he was the
central planner of the wonderful surprises we experienced
over the next five days.

Approximately two hundred of our reunion veterans and spouses attended…requiring the utilization of two hotels in the neighboring larger city of Peterborough. After one day of touring the nearby American Museum and cemetery in Duxford and a visit to beautiful, historic Stamford, we were advised the next day to board the large coaches for the short ride to the site of our old air base at Polebrook…and, we were told we would be having lunch "at a school" in the nearby city of Oundle.

That morning, as our coaches slowly entered the area of our hallowed, granite monuments at Polebrook Airfield, all of us…veterans and spouses, began to experience climactic event after climactic event. In a familiar light drizzle, for a few minutes we milled about taking in the scene. I concentrated on getting the attention of our old commanding officer, former Colonel, and later, Retired Major General Robert Burns. Many of us were pleased to have our pictures taken there at the scene of our service together so many years ago. Following a meaningful ceremony performed by a detail of American servicemen stationed in England, we heard a beautiful prayer delivered by our Chaplain. Then suddenly, David Gower spoke on the PA system asking that we be quiet for a few minutes. Amazingly, in the near distance an evocative sound was heard that every Polebrook veteran recognized: Four Wright Cyclone engines that had to be powering a B-17 Flying Fortress. Indeed, out of the mists, came a once familiar sight…a vintage B-17 flying low banking above us as we began craning our necks upward.

Nostalgia is a powerful emotion. As my wife and I tried to take photographs of that B-17 as it swept three times overhead, I confess that I wept a little. Standing near our English friend, David Gower, I noticed he too was losing a struggle to control his emotions.

Soon it was time to again board the coaches for the short drive to the school in nearby Oundle. We soon came to know of the prestigious reputation of that honored school. In my naivete I had no idea that the Oundle School is an elite boarding school/training ground for many world leaders in politics and industry. Let it be said that we should have taken a hint as we drove through the main street of Oundle. American flags joined by the British Union Jack were flying all along the street and into a lane carrying us through beautiful landscaping to a large meadow. In that meadow stood a massive canopy the size of a circus tent. At a few places the sides were raised that allowed me to see from our coach a mass of people crowded at tables inside. Then we heard music, swing numbers of the forties. As we were in the first coach, my wife, Ginnie and I stepped to the ground following our longtime Association President and wife, Clint and Betty Hammond … and now heard clearly that timeless classic tune "Yankee Doodle". We followed a slightly rising path of some twenty five yards where we were met by city and school officials in formal attire denoting their office…all smiling and murmuring, "thank you, thank you." Each greeter reached out to shake our hands as they directed us to the main opening of the tent structure. The mood was enhanced as the band inside began playing the popular swing music we all remembered from that forever mindful era.

But the most dramatic happening was when we noticed all the people inside at tables, rise then applauded and applauded while we old warriors and spouses walked nodding and crying softly. That welcome, the standing ovation, lasted at least thirty minutes until we all found empty chairs at all those tables partially occupied obviously by an eclectic cross section of locals. The program continued with some emotional, usually witty remarks by English leaders and one distinguished former graduate of the Oundle School. We were eventually served food and drink where we were seated. All quite delicious.

At one point during the meal, and while learning something of each other, my wife and I expressed appreciation for this heartfelt reception. One older, dignified woman at our table put down her wine glass, looked at me kindly, saying, *"You young men sort of left in the middle of the night don't you know, back in 1945. We just didn't have an opportunity to say our farewells…Thank God, that those of us still around, are finally able to say thanks to you and to all those who are gone"*

That spontaneous, emotional thought was a most appropriate ending to the event that day. Also, our conclave of Americans was noteworthy enough for the BBC television to cover the proceedings during most of that momentous week. My wife had the distinction of being one of those interviewed that day by British television.

Closing reunion events that followed the next day were anticlimactic. Finally, it was time to say goodby again. Thus taking busses back to a London Airport and the flight home to the United States. Memories linger of that most memorable journey.

Memorial Site, year 2000, 351st BG Reunion:
Lee Gingery, Public Releations Officer at far right;
In center, Wartime CO of the Group, Retired Major
General, Bob Burns: at his left, Clinton W. Hammond,
Longtime President of our Reunion Association; The
tall man at left in back row is William Montross,
Vice President of our Association.

* * * *

Dedications And Credits

But first, why in the world did I write another book at my age? As a long time fan and long ago as a youngster, an average player of baseball, it is still my favorite team sport. Therefore, I offer what I think is an appropriate metaphor:

I just wanted to stand in the batters box
and take another swing at the baseball
before the game is called!

So thanks to my wonderful wife, Virginia, and all three of our outstanding kids... and their spouses. Lynn, who read most of the manuscript... Scott who was a beacon of encouragement and advice... and Laura, computer smart, and always the helpful one, as with her siblings, senses the needs and requirements of her parents. We are also blessed with four talented grandchildren. Lisa, the eldest helped with the production and performed as a lovely blonde model for pictures, was very much appreciated. All four grandchildren are treasured blessings. Some read manuscript and all helped lead the cheers as we approached the goal of writing *finis* to this project.

Finally, my grateful thanks goes to our local computer guy, Brian Hammons, who was helpful on this project in many ways.

Lee Emerson Gingery